VICTORIAN
MANSION
FLOWER SHOP™
MYSTERIES

Deadhead and Buried

Jan Fields

AnniesFiction.com

Library of Congress-in-Publication Data
Deadhead and Buried / by Jan Fields
p. cm.
I. Title
                    2018942686

AnniesFiction.com
(800) 282-6643
Victorian Mansion Flower Shop Mysteries™
Series Creators: Shari Lohner, Janice Tate
Editor: Elizabeth Morrissey
Cover Illustrator: Bob Kayganich

10 11 12 13 14 | Printed in China | 9 8 7 6 5 4 3 2 1

1

Kaylee Bleu hated leaving her adorable dachshund behind when she went out to eat. Somehow, Bear's big brown eyes always made her feel guilty. Therefore, O'Brien's restaurant was one of Kaylee's favorite spots on Orcas Island, and she was grateful that her friend Mary Bishop had suggested it for dinner. Not only was the food delicious, but the large patio was dog friendly. Bear was a bit of a social butterfly but also well-behaved, so he'd become a favorite at O'Brien's.

As the quiet bustle of diners and servers murmured around them, Kaylee shifted in her seat, careful not to move her ankle, where Bear's warm body pressed against her. It being summer, she didn't exactly need the extra doggy furnace, but she liked knowing where he was.

She peeked across the table over the top of her menu. Mary's head was bowed as she pored over her own menu. Mary had been preoccupied and quiet ever since she'd come back from her trip to the mainland to attend a funeral. Kaylee had done her best to give Mary space—and made doubly sure to keep up her side of the load at her shop, The Flower Patch, where Mary was a part-time florist—but she couldn't help worrying. What if the passing of her friend had made Mary think about retiring? After all, she'd retired once before, leaving her job as dispatcher for the sheriff's department. Mary always said she loved working at The Flower Patch, but that didn't mean she wouldn't decide to give it up for more free time. Kaylee fidgeted nervously. What would she do without Mary's help? When Kaylee's grandmother, Bea Lyons, had owned the shop, she'd relied heavily on Mary, and when Kaylee took over the business, she did the same.

Kaylee's worry certainly hadn't decreased when Mary nervously asked Kaylee to join her for dinner so they could talk. *Please don't tell me you're going to quit*, Kaylee begged silently. She would be completely lost without Mary's help.

Kaylee felt the pressure on her ankle shift, and she smiled down at Bear, who was particularly handsome this evening in his bright blue bow tie. Kaylee knew that the little dog had noticed Mary's change in mood as well. He was acting unusually reserved around Mary, and it probably wasn't because she smelled like her new kitten, Lily. In fact, Kaylee hadn't seen Bear beg Mary for a treat in days. Since the dachshund's one true weakness was dog cookies, his hesitance to beg spoke volumes about Mary's odd behavior. As nervous as Kaylee felt about whatever bombshell Mary planned to drop on her, a part of her would be glad when it was over.

To Kaylee's surprise, the warm pressure on her ankle lifted, and Bear scooted to the limits of his leash and gave one sharp bark. Kaylee recognized it as his greeting. He'd clearly spotted someone he knew, and, judging by the wild wagging of his tail, it was someone he liked a lot. Kaylee followed his gaze and immediately spotted Deputy Nick Durham leading a lovely young woman by the hand.

Kaylee smiled. The charming sheriff's deputy always made a fuss over Bear whenever he saw him. It was no wonder he was one of Bear's favorite people.

True to form, Nick turned at the sound of Bear's bark and waved at Mary and Kaylee. "I see you ladies have a handsome date for dinner," he called, gesturing at Bear.

"I wouldn't want Herb thinking Bear is moving in on his lady," Kaylee said, "so I'd best claim Bear as my date."

Mary laughed. "Don't worry. Herb doesn't mind sharing

my affections with Bear."

The little dog sat up on his haunches and pawed the air, one of his standby tricks for getting attention.

Nick's date clapped her hands together. "He is adorable. I'd love to get a little dog. I'm sure he's wonderful company." She beamed at Nick. "Don't you think that would be great? I love animals. Honestly, I'd live in a zoo if I was able."

"Oh no," Nick said in mock alarm. "I'd better get you to our table before he charms you away from me." He wagged a finger at Bear as if warning him off.

Bear sat up and pawed the air again, not intimidated in the least.

Kaylee laughed. If there was one person on Orcas Island—or in the entire state of Washington, for that matter—who couldn't point fingers at anyone else for charming others, it was Nick Durham. He was a good guy, but an absolutely incorrigible flirt.

Nick grinned back at Kaylee, almost as if he read her thoughts in her expression. "Have a nice evening, ladies," he said, then led his date away. The young woman cast one last glance over her shoulder at Bear, appearing almost wistful.

Bear seemed disappointed that he hadn't gotten any petting out of the encounter. He trotted back to his position at Kaylee's side and flopped down on the end of her foot with a sigh. Kaylee glanced across the table at Mary, only to see her waving at someone else.

Jessica and Luke Roberts stood at the edge of the patio, waving back at Mary. Kaylee raised a hand in greeting as Jessica towed Luke over to their table. As always, they made a handsome couple. Though nearly ten years older than Kaylee, Jessica—with her coal-black hair and her brown eyes usually alight with excitement—seemed the same age or younger. She owned Death by Chocolate, the bakery next to The Flower Patch, and her sparkling personality helped make the dessert shop a Turtle Cove favorite. Luke, a tax accountant, had a quieter nature, radiating a kind of strong stability that always struck Kaylee as a nice contrast to Jessica's energy and enthusiasm.

As soon as they reached the table, Jessica took Mary's hand. "I haven't seen you since you got back to the island. I was beginning to think you'd lost your love for my coffee." Jessica's tone was teasing, but then her smile faded. "I'm so sorry to hear about your friend."

Mary's return smile was strained. "Thank you. It was a difficult time, but I'm glad to be home again."

Glad to be home, Kaylee thought, *but clearly still upset.*

"And we're glad to have you back." Jessica widened her eyes in mock alarm. "Especially with the summer teen program about to begin."

"Why don't you and Luke join us?" Mary suggested. "I'd love to hear what you're going to do with the kids. It was wonderful of you to take on so much of the work for the program."

Kaylee nearly frowned as Jessica thanked Mary for the invitation and Luke pulled out a chair. Was Mary going to include Jessica and Luke in whatever talk she'd invited Kaylee out to have? Or was this Mary chickening out? *That's it*, Kaylee thought despairingly. *She's planning to quit. Why else would she put off telling me? What am I going to do?*

"Did you know Nick Durham has a new girlfriend?" Mary asked, nodding in the direction of Nick's table.

"I did," Jessica said. "She looks just like Kaylee."

Startled, Kaylee turned toward Nick's table. His date was slender with long, straight dark brown hair, so she supposed that was a similarity. However, while Kaylee's skin tone was more olive, Nick's date had a golden-brown tan that probably faded in the winter. "I don't really see it," she said.

"Of course you don't. We never see ourselves quite the way other people see us," Jessica said lightly, but immediately returned to the topic of Nick's date. "Her name is Felicia Lewis. She's been in Death by Chocolate several times. And not always with Nick."

"That's not shocking," Kaylee said. "His job takes up a lot of his time."

"Perhaps," Jessica said, her eyes sparkling. "But she used to come in with Isaac Pine, and they were definitely close."

"I don't know that name," Kaylee said.

"He's one of the summer people," Mary explained. "He's been in The Flower Patch a few times over the years, usually to pick up flowers when his parents were visiting the island. His mother loves entertaining. I don't think his parents summer on Orcas Island anymore, though. Isaac is a quiet sort, but always very polite."

"And rich," Luke put in, making everyone stare at him in surprise. Luke normally ignored the conversation if it tended toward gossip. His face reddened. "I happen to know his family's land here is of interest to developers. It's quite an extensive piece of property."

"Ugh." Mary pulled a face. "Developers are the bane of the islands. They can turn a beautiful village into some kind of tourist theme park."

"I think that's the goal, generally," Jessica said.

"I wouldn't worry about that piece of land." Luke waved a hand dismissively. "I'm fairly sure the Pines have no interest in letting it go." His gaze fell on Nick's table for the first time, and he frowned. "And as much as I like Nick, I strongly disapprove of anyone moving in on someone else's girlfriend. Isaac Pine seems like a good sort."

"We don't know that Nick did anything like that," Kaylee said loyally. Though Nick's flirting could be mildly annoying, she liked him. He was a good deputy, and he'd certainly helped her more than once. "That doesn't sound like him."

"I don't know about that," Jessica said. "He *is* a flirt. Though I do like Felicia. She seems very sweet."

"She liked Bear." In Kaylee's book, anyone who appreciated her beloved dog certainly got the benefit of the doubt.

"Well, if Nick has stolen someone's girl, he may end up with a punch in the nose," Luke said. "I like Nick, but where women are concerned, I'm not sure he's entirely blameless."

"I think we're in for a major crisis." Jessica sighed. "Oliver has been very droopy lately. I think we're going to see some kind of storm coming." She gazed pointedly at Nick's table. "And that might be the eye of the storm right there."

Kaylee smiled at the dramatic prediction. Oliver was Jessica's lavender geranium, and her friend was convinced that Oliver was psychic. She often saw omens in every drooping leaf or wilted petal. Coupled with her love of conspiracy theories, it was no wonder she saw dire warnings regarding Nick's dating life.

The server arrived to take their orders, and Kaylee was glad their conversation was interrupted. She felt guilty gossiping about Nick. She was pleased that a new topic came up after they'd placed their dinner requests.

As the server left their table, Jessica turned pointedly to Mary. "Are you going to be able to help out with the Learners on Location program?" Jessica asked, referring to the teen project she'd mentioned earlier.

"Of course," Mary said. "Kaylee signed the shop up for a tutorial on the basics of flower arranging. We'll tag team so she can share botanical information on all the flowers."

"Just what every teen boy wants to know," Luke muttered.

Jessica poked him. "Every teen doesn't have to try every project. And some of the boys might like flower arranging."

Luke shrugged. "It's too bad Reese is at a conference on the mainland. I'm sure he would do a project that's geared a little more toward the boys."

"Again, some boys might *like* flower arranging," Kaylee said. "There are lots of male designers. But if you must know, Reese is going to be back in time to do a program on making things from found and recycled objects, which might be of interest to both the boys and the girls. And Nick is doing a demonstration on animal tracks. So you needn't worry about the poor, bored boys."

"I'll have to remind DeeDee about Reese's program," Jessica said. "She might want to sneak the girls in. Polly and Zoe both love pounding nails." Along with Kaylee, Jessica, and Mary, DeeDee Wilcox was the fourth member of the Petal Pushers, the garden club that had taken on the Learners on Location project.

Luke raised his hands in mock defeat. "I stand corrected. You've clearly got more than enough interesting things for all the kids."

When their food arrived, conversation continued about the program and other summer projects the club might take on. Summer was a busy time on Orcas Island, with lots of people coming and going. Some, like Isaac Pine, lived across Puget Sound in Seattle and had seasonal homes on the island, but others simply visited for the charm and beauty. Though Turtle Cove was one of the smaller villages on Orcas, it offered breathtaking scenery, quaint and sometimes quirky shops, and plenty of things to do and see. Small businesses around town took visitors on whale-watching cruises and rented everything from kayaks and sailboats to bicycles.

About the time they were discussing whether anyone had room for dessert, Nick and Felicia arrived at the table, stopping on their way out. Nick bent to offer Bear a pat on the head, then introduced Felicia.

"We've met at Death by Chocolate," Jessica said, offering the young woman her lovely smile. "Nice to see you, Felicia."

"I love your bakery." Felicia patted her flat stomach. "Although it will get me into trouble if I'm not careful."

"I know the feeling," Kaylee said.

"Kaylee and Mary are at The Flower Patch," Nick said to Felicia. "And they're all in that gardening group I told you about, the Petal Pushers." He turned to Kaylee. "Felicia is crazy about flowers, and I thought she might be able to visit your group. Could she sit in on a meeting?"

Felicia's cheeks were reddening from all the attention. "I do love flowers," the blushing woman said, almost shyly. "There seem to be so many in bloom here."

"You should see Kaylee's house," Nick said. "Her backyard is all wildflowers and lavender. The smell is amazing."

Felicia reddened still more, probably worried that Nick was trying a bit too hard to push her into the group. "It sounds lovely."

"You should come by the shop," Mary suggested warmly. "We're going to be demonstrating flower arranging as part of a summer program for teens from the mainland. We would love to have another hand to help with the kids if you're interested."

Felicia brightened at the invitation. "That sounds like fun, though I don't know how much help I'll be. I can pass out ribbons or something, but I'd be right there with the teens hanging on your every word. I'd love to learn more about flower arranging."

"Then we'll plan on your coming," Mary said, and she gave the young woman the details for the demonstration.

Just as Mary finished briefing Felicia, a strange man walked up to their table, his gaze so fixed on Felicia that Kaylee doubted he even noticed any of the rest of them. The man was tall and slender, with close-cropped blond hair and freckles. His eyes were very blue and his mouth was set in a thin line.

He caught Felicia by the arm. "I need to talk to you," he told her. "Right now."

Nick grabbed the man's wrist, just above where he held Felicia's arm. "Back off, Pine."

Kaylee realized the man must be Felicia's former boyfriend, Isaac Pine. Judging by his serious expression as he stared back at Nick, he wasn't done with the relationship. Bear growled deep in his chest, upset by his friend's angry voice. Kaylee scooted her chair back slightly and scooped Bear up to quiet him.

"This has nothing to do with you, Deputy Durham," Isaac said. Though he had let go of Felicia's arm, he gazed at her intensely over Nick's shoulder. "You need to talk to me. Now."

"That's it," Nick said, twisting Isaac's arm behind him. "You're out of here!"

Bear barked once as Nick wrestled the man away from the table.

"Nick!" Felicia gasped, but the deputy didn't look at her as he marched his detainee toward the edge of the patio, leaving Felicia staring after the men with wide, frightened eyes.

2

For a moment, it seemed as if the whole restaurant was frozen by the conflict they'd just seen. Then Mary stood up and spoke gently to Felicia. "Would you like to sit with us while you wait for Nick?"

Felicia faced the table, then managed a weak smile. "No, thank you. I should probably go after them." Her voice sounded less than convinced, but she turned to follow them just as Nick stepped back on the patio.

"Here he comes," Jessica said with forced cheer.

Mary sank back into her seat. Kaylee wasn't sure if it was safe to put Bear back down. Nick's face was still red with emotion.

As soon as he reached them, he took Felicia's hand. "It's okay. Isaac's gone."

Felicia snatched her hand back. "You didn't have to be so aggressive with him. What's wrong with you?"

Nick gaped at her. "What's wrong with *me*?"

Her face dark, Felicia stepped around him and stalked off. Nick quickly followed, leaving an awkward silence in his wake.

Mary finally broke the ensuing silence. "Wow. That was dramatic."

"You know," Luke said, "I think you ought to rethink the belief that Nick wouldn't move in on another guy's girlfriend, because it certainly looked to me like there's bad blood between him and Isaac."

"That doesn't mean Nick took his girlfriend," Kaylee argued. "Though I do think Isaac still has feelings for her." She gave Bear a squeeze and set him back down by her chair.

To Kaylee's relief, their server immediately approached to ask if anyone wanted dessert. Since they were all full, Mary just asked for the check. Kaylee noticed her voice sounded as relieved as Kaylee felt. This had certainly been an unusual dinner.

"I can bring some flowers from my garden for your Learners on Location demonstration," Jessica offered while they waited for their server to return. "I know flowers can be expensive, and I have some lovely ones blooming. The zinnias and dahlias are especially impressive this year."

Kaylee smiled, grateful for the donation and the change in topic. "That's so nice of you. I'm going to cut some *Daucus carota* from my garden as well. The lacy texture is a wonderful addition to so many arrangements."

"I know that one," Luke said. "Wild carrot."

"I like the name Queen Anne's lace better," Jessica said. "Makes it sound regal. We have some of that growing wild, but I like the more colorful flowers for my beds."

Kaylee found herself relaxing with the talk of plants. As a trained botanist, there was really no topic that felt more natural to her. She loved everything about plants: their complexity, the amazing way they adapted to their environments, and their benefits to mankind—an area she felt had barely been tapped. She was glad to be out of the cutthroat world of academia that had consumed her entire life before her move to Orcas Island, but she still loved reading about the research others were doing.

"What day did you say Reese was coming back?" Jessica asked, breaking into Kaylee's musings. "I need to talk to him about an irrigation system for my garden."

"I can put that in," Luke protested.

Jessica chuckled. "Right. I think I heard that last year when I first started talking about it." She squeezed his hand to soften the criticism. "You do plenty around the house. I don't think you have the time for such a big project."

"In answer to your question, Jess, Reese is coming back on the Thursday morning ferry," Kaylee added.

"It's certainly helpful that you know Reese's schedule so well," Mary said, her voice slightly teasing.

"It's just because I helped with the scheduling of the Learners on Location presentations before he left," Kaylee replied, a little defensively. "I had to make sure we scheduled his presentation on upcycled furniture for when he would actually be on the island."

"Right." Jessica's tone was similar to Mary's. "You had to know for purely organizational reasons."

"Now, Jess," Luke scolded. "Don't tease. You're making Kaylee blush."

Kaylee put up a palm to cool her warm cheek as the server returned. She was grateful as the conversation changed to dividing up the check. She would cheerfully have paid it all just to keep them off the topic of Reese. He was a good friend, and Kaylee enjoyed his company very much, but the Petal Pushers seemed insistent on turning it into something romantic.

The group broke up after the check was paid, and Kaylee walked out to the parking lot with Mary by her side and Bear in her arms. Mary reached over and gave the little dog's ears a scratch, sending his tail wagging. "He was certainly a good boy this evening."

Kaylee agreed. "I'll have to give him an extra treat when we get home."

When they arrived at their cars, Mary touched Kaylee's arm. "Can I ask a favor of you?"

"Of course," Kaylee said, wondering if Mary was finally going to spill what was bothering her. Her stomach tensed. *Don't quit, please.* "Anything."

Mary laced her fingers together and stared down at her

hands. "The funeral that Herb and I went to was terrible, and it wasn't just because I miss my old friend." She sighed deeply. "As I sat there during the service, I realized none of the choices really seemed right for Anne. She was such a lively person, and she would have hated the choice of music. I know she would. And the floral arrangements had several flowers she hated because they triggered her allergies."

"That's too bad," Kaylee said sympathetically, wondering how this could possibly relate to a favor.

"After the funeral, when I talked to Anne's family" —again Mary sighed—"half the family seemed furious with the other half. There was this ugly fight, and the most awful things were said. It was horrible. Anne would have been heartbroken to hear it." She raised her eyes to Kaylee's. "I don't want that."

"I'm sure that won't happen," Kaylee said gently. "And that's a long time in the future. You're still young and in good health. You don't need to worry about a funeral."

"I'm sure Anne thought that too," Mary said. "That's the problem: It always seems a long way off until the time comes. I want to make sure nothing like that happens when I'm gone. So I've decided to plan my funeral."

Kaylee's eyes widened. "Really? How does Herb feel about that?"

"Well, at first he wasn't in favor of the plan at all. Now he's come around. Mostly. He's okay with helping me pick music and things like that." She stopped and took a deep breath, giving Kaylee the sense that she was about to reveal the favor. "But he has completely refused to come with me to pick out a casket."

"Oh." Kaylee could see why Herb would feel that way. She was a bit creeped out by the idea. *Who would want to look at caskets knowing they would be inside one someday?*

"I want to square away *all* the details," Mary said. "Still, I hate the idea of doing it by myself."

Kaylee had a sinking feeling about where this was going, and it was confirmed by Mary's next words.

"Would you go with me? I have an appointment with Giles on Tuesday afternoon." Giles Akin was the local coroner, and he also ran Akin Funeral Chapel with his wife, Thelma, and their son, Jay.

Kaylee squirmed a little inside, but she knew that Mary would do her the same favor, and she'd always been there for Kaylee's grandmother as well. Kaylee forced a smile, hoping it came across at least halfway natural. "Of course, Mary. You know I'd do anything for you."

A bright smile blossomed on Mary's face, and she threw her arms around Kaylee. Bear was squeezed into the hug and licked both of their faces, his tail whipping back and forth.

"Thank you," Mary said. "I know it's a lot to ask, but I'll feel so much better once this plan is in place. Honestly, this has been bothering me so much."

"I could tell something was troubling you," Kaylee said. "I'm just glad it's something I can help with." And she meant it. Mary's expression suggested that a huge weight had come off her shoulders. Sure, it was probably going to be an uncomfortable few hours, but it would be well worth it to give her friend some peace of mind.

On Monday morning, Kaylee stood gazing out the windows of her home, Wildflower Cottage, absolutely dazzled by the beauty of the view. The plantings close to the cottage were lovely, but the fields of lavender never failed to delight her. "We live in the best place in the world," she said to Bear, who woofed as if in agreement.

She'd woken early, feeling full of energy. The weather was pleasant and sunny, so Kaylee decided to bike to The Flower Patch. She wanted to feel the tingle of muscles well used, and the exercise would invigorate her. She didn't spend enough time enjoying the beauty of the island face-to-face, rather than through the protective shell of her car.

"How about an adventure today?" she asked Bear, who wore a jaunty polka-dot bow tie that Kaylee had picked out to match her mood. Unsurprisingly, he yipped and raced around her excitedly.

Kaylee wheeled the bicycle out of the shed and hooked Bear's harness into the doggy seat. The little dog sat patiently as she made sure he was secure, though his tail wagged hard, thumping rhythmically against the seat. "I know," Kaylee said. "I'm excited too." She swung a leg over the bike and set off.

Since it was early morning, the road into town was empty, giving Kaylee plenty of opportunity to admire the quiet countryside. Closer to town, the road would hug the coastline on one side, but at the beginning of Kaylee's ride, the passing scenery was a mix of sparse woodland lined with mostly firs, cedars, and madrone trees, all evergreen. That meant the view was this beautiful all year round. Now and then, she'd pass one of the small summer cottages rented to guests who wanted a quiet spot in the trees.

As she pedaled, Kaylee realized that her stressful past life as a plant taxonomy professor at the University of Washington felt very far away. Surrounded as she was by nature these days, the life of an academic felt almost like a dream she'd had, and not always a pleasant one. She'd had good friends at the university, people who insisted she'd miss the intellectual challenge of academia. True, she did miss some things, but she was certain she'd gained much more than she'd lost.

While she was caught up in her thoughts, a car had joined her on the road, though far behind her. The sound of the roaring engine finally cut through her musings. She glanced in the mirror clipped to her handlebars, but the road was so hilly that she couldn't see the car clearly. "If I can't see him," she murmured, "he might not see me."

Bear must have heard her voice and picked up on her nervousness, because he whined anxiously.

Now that she was paying attention, Kaylee could tell the car coming up behind her was going very fast. She moved as far to the side of the road as she could to give the car plenty of room to pass. She was closer than she liked to the ditch, but with the car coming up so quickly, she thought the driver might be surprised to find her on the road at all, and she wanted to be sure he had plenty of time to react. She'd heard from people in town that guests to the island didn't always share the road as well as one would like.

The speeding car crested the last hill between it and Kaylee. In moments, the car roared by her, but it was too close to the shoulder. Kaylee turned sharply to avoid being clipped by one of the sedan's side mirrors. The movement ran her right off the road and into the ditch, pitching Kaylee off the bike. The car never stopped or even slowed down, and it was out of sight before Kaylee could get back on her feet.

Bear barked excitedly as Kaylee righted the bike and checked him over. "Are you all right?" she asked, brushing dirt and specks of brush from his coat. Bear's response was to lick her cheek. She laughed. "I'll take that as a yes. That was far too close for comfort, wasn't it, boy?"

Kaylee unbuckled Bear from the seat and took him for a short walk in the stand of trees near the road. She needed the time to recover from the near accident before getting back on the bike.

Bear enthusiastically took the opportunity to sniff around trees and in holes. "At least one of us is having a great time," Kaylee said.

When her knees no longer felt wobbly and her hands stopped shaking, Kaylee buckled Bear back into the seat and headed off again for town. She would no longer be at work early, but she knew Mary would understand once she heard the details. Kaylee wished she'd gotten a glimpse of the car's driver or even a bit of the license plate. "Not that I'd go to the police," she muttered. She spoke to the police often enough and doubted they would do much about the driver. After all, he hadn't hit her.

"I should stop saying 'he,'" Kaylee said aloud to Bear. "I suppose it could have been a woman as easily as a man. It was probably just someone who wasn't paying attention. It's not like that car was aiming for me." On the other hand, it had been very close—too close. She had trouble believing a driver wouldn't have seen her. And now that she thought about it, had the vehicle actually swerved toward her?

Don't be silly, Kaylee.

With a sigh, she realized that the encounter had ruined her enjoyment of the beautiful morning. If she let it, she suspected it would make her jumpy about riding the bike on the island. "And that would just be ridiculous. There's nothing to be afraid of out here."

But Kaylee had a nervous flutter in her stomach that lasted all the way to town.

3

As she got within half a mile of Turtle Cove's Main Street shops, the road ran closer to the shore. Now, Kaylee could see the ocean, already dotted with early morning sailboats. With the sound of the surf in her ears and the fresh breeze off the sea, Kaylee slowly felt the tension seep from her muscles, though she doubted she would really relax until she reached the shop. Every time a car passed her on the road, she felt a fresh flutter of nerves.

When she rode by the town park, Bear barked several times at the sight of one of his favorite places. Kaylee was glad to see Bear had already put their frightful experience behind him. The little dog certainly knew how to live in the moment. *I wish I could do that.* Kaylee stopped the bike to let a car pass and patted Bear on the head. "Maybe later we'll make it to the dog park."

She turned off Shoreline Drive and onto Main Street, where The Flower Patch stood like a stately matriarch, welcoming passersby inside. The charming Victorian mansion had a wraparound porch complete with white wooden rockers and wicker tables that beckoned to anyone who might like a spot to rest and watch the little town's hustle and bustle. Hanging baskets of flowers added a burst of cheerful color to the porch. The beautiful old mansion felt almost as much like home to Kaylee as her cottage did, and finally she felt the last cobwebs of fear blow from her mind.

She parked the bike in a nearby rack, looping a chain and lock through the frame. She freed Bear from his seat, and he wiggled all over with delight. He loved The Flower Patch as much as Kaylee did. Kaylee left his harness in the seat and snapped a leash to his collar. "Let's go see Mary."

She certainly didn't have to tell Bear twice. He tugged her forward, his nails skittering on the sidewalk as he strained to reach the steps up to the front door.

As Kaylee had expected, Mary stood behind the counter near the cash register. She turned her attention from a clipboard in her hand and smiled. "You look a bit windblown."

Kaylee reached up with one hand to touch her hair. She had pulled it back into a ponytail, but she could feel errant strands. She suspected the tumble off the bike had rumpled her far more than the wind. "I'm sorry I'm late. I biked in."

"Oh, that must have been a lovely ride," Mary said. "And you aren't really late. You only missed our visiting romantic." Kaylee knew the young man Mary meant. He'd come in every morning to buy a flower for his wife during their stay. Each day it was something different. "You should run next door for a cup of coffee. No rush."

Kaylee hesitated, knowing Mary would want to hear about her experience on the road, but she could practically hear the coffee calling her. "You're a darling," she said finally. "I'll be right back." She pointed at Bear. "Be good for Mary."

Bear trotted behind the counter, knowing Mary would give him a treat as soon as Kaylee left.

"Only one biscuit," Kaylee warned Mary. "Plump is not a good condition for dachshunds. It's hard on their spines."

"I think Bear is a bit too lively for a few treats to make him chubby."

Not that he wouldn't like to test that theory. Kaylee slipped out of the shop, trotted down the steps, and headed next door to Death by Chocolate.

Jessica was fussing over Oliver as Kaylee entered. The anxious expression on Jessica's face resolved into her usual warm smile. "Coffee?"

"Yes please." Kaylee stood at the counter and examined Oliver. The lavender geranium really was lovely, and Jessica did a good job of not smothering the little plant with too much love. Too many houseplant owners watered their darlings to death or burned them up with fertilizer in the desire to make sure they were well. Jessica had made up a rich inner life for Oliver, but she definitely handled his actual care well. "Oliver is looking good."

"You think so?" Jessica asked studying the plant anxiously. "I was thinking that his color is a bit off."

"He's lovely."

"Thanks." Jessica set Kaylee's coffee on the counter, then reached out and picked a leaf from Kaylee's shoulder. She held it out. "Casual Monday?"

"Not intentionally." Kaylee recapped her accident quickly, ending with, "Summer guests really need to remember they're not in the city anymore."

"Tell me about it!" a voice boomed from behind Kaylee, making her jump. She turned to see Roz Corzo, the owner of Corzo Whale Watch. Kaylee hadn't noticed Roz nursing a cup of coffee at one of the tables near the window, but the ship captain certainly couldn't resist indulging in one of her favorite pastimes: complaining about the summer people.

Kaylee cast an apologetic glance toward Jessica and mouthed, "Sorry."

Roz leaned on the counter so she could launch into her tale. "You should have seen this couple I took on a private whale watch a week ago Sunday. There we were, in one of the most beautiful places in the world on a perfect day. But do you think they paid a lick of attention?"

Jessica smiled slightly. "I'm going to guess not."

"You know it," Roz said. "They spent the whole time with their heads together, talking. And they sat as far from me as they could get."

Kaylee had to smother a grin at that. She wasn't one to indulge in catty thoughts, but standing as close to Roz as she was, she couldn't miss the strong smell of fish coming from the captain. She couldn't help but wonder whether that had been the cause of the couple's distance.

Roz must have caught the smile because she responded with a glare. "I had to fill my bait buckets this morning. I'm taking some fishermen out later. I didn't smell like fish on the whale watch. Those two were just city folks. They barely even reacted when I pointed out a whole pod of orcas."

"Did they pay all right?" Jessica asked, her voice unnaturally innocent. "Give a tip?"

"Yes," Roz growled. "But that's not the point. They could have saved their money and stayed home for all the attention they paid."

"Did they complain about the trip?" Kaylee asked. "Maybe they were expecting something different?"

"No, I'll give them that," Roz said. Kaylee could practically see the woman's ruffled feathers beginning to settle. "I've had worse clients."

"I'm sure you have," Kaylee said sympathetically.

Roz narrowed her eyes at Kaylee. "You know, now that I think about it, the woman looked a lot like you. Except prettier."

Ouch.

"Maybe it was Felicia Lewis," Jessica suggested. "Though then you would have known the man since she's dating Nick Durham."

Roz barked out a laugh. "It wasn't Nick. It was Isaac Pine. His family has been coming to Orcas Island forever. Bunch of rich summer dolts who don't know what they want. You should have heard the group I took out this last Saturday. One of the women actually complained because I couldn't make the whales jump for the camera. Like I have them trained or something." She shook her head at the memory and slugged down the last of her coffee. "Well, I'd better get back to the boat. Who knows what the fishermen I'm taking out today will do?" She stomped out of the shop.

"Sounds like Isaac and Felicia were really close before Nick came along," Kaylee said after the door closed behind Roz. She found the thought uncomfortable. "I really don't believe Nick would steal someone's girlfriend."

Jessica lifted a shoulder in a small shrug. "Maybe he didn't mean to. You know Nick. He flirts with everyone. It's like breathing for him. Maybe he charmed her away accidentally."

"You make him sound like a wizard." Kaylee suddenly felt guilty gossiping about Nick. She shifted and raised her coffee cup to her lips to cover her discomfort.

To her surprise, Jessica gasped and pointed to her arm. "Kaylee! You're bleeding."

Kaylee glanced down to see what had alarmed her friend. Her sleeve had fallen away when she lifted her mug, and there was a long scrape running down her forearm. "Oh, I knew it stung, but I didn't realize it had broken the skin."

"Let me get the first aid kit and fix you up."

"It's okay," Kaylee said. "I have a kit at The Flower Patch."

If Jessica heard her, she didn't listen. She brought out a white box with a red cross on the cover and promptly pulled out antiseptic and bandages. "You should report the car to the police," Jessica said. "Before he manages to hurt someone else."

"I don't want to make a big deal out of one unfortunate accident," Kaylee said softly, wincing at the sting as Jessica cleaned the scrape with an antiseptic wipe. "It's not like he actually hit me. I just overreacted."

"The driver was probably texting," Jessica grumbled. "I'm stunned by how many times I see drivers with phones in their hand."

"Could be."

Intellectually, Kaylee knew the incident was certainly something like that, but the vague feeling that the driver had actually veered toward her persisted. It was probably just a reaction to the shock and terror of the moment. No one would have any reason to *try* to run her over. Would they?

Shaking off her disquiet, she stood still as Jessica finished bandaging her arm. "Thanks for the doctoring. I should get back to the shop. It's bad enough that I got to work late. I don't need Mary thinking I'm not coming to work at all. Especially since she's been kind of down since her friend Anne's funeral."

"I'd noticed that too," Jessica said. "But she's better today. Maybe having dinner with all of us last night helped. We're a cheering group."

"For sure." Kaylee had been so distracted by her near accident that she'd barely noticed Mary's mood. Her friend had seemed a little more talkative. Kaylee hoped Mary was feeling better. What she'd really like was if Mary felt so much better that she dropped the whole idea of shopping for coffins.

"She came in here for her morning coffee, and she was humming," Jessica said. "I think just being around her might have perked Oliver up a bit. What do you think?" She gently poked at the soil around the geranium's stem.

"I think he's doing just fine. He is very well-loved." Kaylee thanked Jessica again for the doctoring, paid for her coffee, and headed back to the shop.

As predicted, Mary was much more her usual cheerful self—though she noticed the large bandage on Kaylee's arm immediately. "Does that have any connection to the grass under Bear's collar?"

When Kaylee explained what had happened, Mary was indignant that someone would come so close to hurting her friend. "I wonder if we should have some work done on that road. It sounds like the brush needs to be cleared away from the shoulders. The road is popular with bikers and joggers, and clearly it's too easy for someone to get hurt."

"The shoulder is much wider and clearer closer to town, which is really where most of the bikers and joggers are," Kaylee said. "I was just caught out in one of the wilder spots."

"That just means we need to make sure the shoulders are kept up out your way as well." She frowned at Kaylee's arm. "That is simply unacceptable."

Kaylee was touched by Mary's display of concern. "I really do think it was a freak accident. And I'm fine. So is Bear. Right, boy?"

Hearing his name, Bear sat up and barked, making both women laugh.

Mary reached out and patted Kaylee's unwounded arm. "I'm glad you're okay. I wanted to thank you again for agreeing to come with me to the funeral home tomorrow. I know it's not exactly a pleasure outing, but it is such a relief to know I don't have to handle it alone."

Kaylee felt a little guilty for hoping Mary would give up on the idea. She realized it was her agreement that had lifted Mary's mood so much. "If it will give you peace of mind, then I'm happy to help. We'll need to close a little early tomorrow to make it to the appointment on time, so we'd best dive in and make sure we're caught up on orders."

They were going through an unusual lull. They had a stack of small orders, but during the summer, they were often crazy busy doing wedding flowers. Kaylee loved the summer rush, when the cases were full of colorful blooms and it seemed every corner of the shop was bursting with life. Bear loved it too, though mostly for the steady flow of customers who usually seemed ready to give attention to a certain friendly dachshund.

Kaylee stood in front of one of the refrigerated cases and took a deep breath, slipping into her creative place and finally shrugging off the last of her nerves. She thought about the arrangement she would make first. The order had been called in by a nervous-sounding young man who was coming to the island with his wife for their first wedding anniversary. "I want something dramatic," he'd said. "Michaela is very dramatic. And she loves lilies, especially the big showy ones. Do you know what I mean? Don't make all the flowers lilies, but put those in it. And her favorite colors are pink and white, but bright pink. Okay?"

It was completely okay. Kaylee had ordered in a selection of *Lilium orientalis* and *Lilium asiaticum* that fit the description. She had also found some lovely roses that exactly matched the darkest shade of pink on the stargazers.

She selected the most dramatic lilies and the fullest roses. Then she eyed her greenery, hunting for the perfect dark green that could hold its own with the striking flowers. While she worked, she hummed softly. Remembering Jessica's remark about Mary's humming, she chuckled softly. She and Mary were clearly back to their normal, sunny selves.

With the return of her cheerful energy, Kaylee was able to finish nearly all the orders on her half of the list in record time. She was staring into the coolers for inspiration for her last bouquet when Mary tapped her on the shoulder.

"Sorry to startle you," Mary said when Kaylee jumped, "but I thought you wanted to meet the ferry today. For the Learners on Location kids?"

"Oh right." Kaylee's gaze flashed to the clock on the wall.

"I'll have to hustle. Do you want to come, Bear?"

The little dog had been dozing under the worktable, but he scurried out, tail wagging eagerly at the promise of going somewhere.

Kaylee laughed at the excitement in his bright eyes. "I'll take that as a yes."

The day was as bright and beautiful as the early morning had been, with a breeze coming off the water to cool the heat from the summer sun. Bear pranced along beside Kaylee with his head up, watching the passersby carefully for signs of potential petting. As they passed Death by Chocolate, Kaylee spotted Jessica and waved. She loved feeling a part of the island and surrounded by friends.

Across the street, she saw Felicia coming out of The Chic Boutique with a shopping bag. Since she was so full of warm feelings about the island, Kaylee passed a little of that warmth along by waving at Felicia and calling out her name. Felicia looked up in surprise, then delight. The other woman waved back and hurried across the street, causing a driver to honk at her in annoyance.

"Hi," Felicia said as she reached Kaylee and Bear. "You're Kaylee, right? Nick says nice things about you."

"Good memory," Kaylee answered. "I'm sure you've met a lot of people since you came to the island. Nick knows everyone."

"He does. I expect that's a side effect of his job." Felicia squatted to pet Bear. "And I definitely remember this handsome guy. Hi, Bear."

"You've got a friend for life now. He loves attention."

"How could I resist? And I love the bow tie. He's just adorable."

Bear's tail wagged so hard that his entire back half seemed to wiggle along with it, making both Kaylee and Felicia laugh.

"I wish I had a treat for you," Felicia said, and Bear's ears lifted slightly at the word.

"If there's one thing Bear doesn't need more of, it's treats. Mary spoils him shamelessly."

"I met her at the restaurant too, right? She was the older lady with the lovely smile."

"You *do* have a good memory," Kaylee said.

"I try." Felicia stood. "Are you heading for the waterfront? I was going to go down and watch the waves for a while. I find that so peaceful. May I walk along with you?"

"Of course. I'm on my way to meet the ferry."

Felicia fell in beside Kaylee, and they continued on with Bear prancing between them. "Do you have a friend coming in on the ferry?" Felicia asked.

"I hope so, though not anyone I've met yet," Kaylee answered, earning a confused expression from Felicia. She grinned and explained about her errand to meet the Learners on Location group.

Felicia nodded. "Oh, I remember. Nick said something about them when we met you last night. I think that's a wonderful idea. Everyone on the island seems so generous and kind. I just love it. I could see myself living here forever."

"I fell in love with the island when I used to come visit my grandparents," Kaylee said. "It took me a while to realize it was where I wanted to live, but now I can't imagine being anywhere else."

"It feels so safe." Felicia's gaze swept the area ahead, her expression dreamy.

Kaylee agreed that the island was quite safe, but she thought it was an odd thing to focus on. *What kind of place must Felicia be from?* "Are you from Seattle?"

If Felicia heard her, she didn't answer the question, instead pointing ahead. "Look. Is that an eagle?"

Kaylee followed Felicia's finger to see a bald eagle fly down to scoop something from the water. "Amazing, aren't they?" she said. "I'm told we have nesting pairs on the island."

"It's magical," Felicia whispered. "I love birds. Imagine being able to simply fly away whenever you wanted."

Kaylee examined the other woman's face and realized why Nick was so taken with her. She seemed like the sort of person who put a lot of herself into every moment. It was a very appealing quality.

"Nick might know where you can see the eagle nests," Kaylee suggested, "though you don't want to get too close because then the parents might abandon the nest. The eaglets aren't exactly cute because they look kind of angry, but I think they're fascinating. I heard someone has a nest camera set up, but I haven't visited the website."

"I'll have to ask Nick," Felicia said. "There isn't much about the island that he doesn't know. He's an amazing tour guide."

"And a great deputy too," Kaylee agreed.

"I don't doubt that. I think being a deputy has made him a bit overprotective though. He doesn't like that I'm staying in this sweet little cabin with woods all around. But I like it. It's snug, and it's not like I can't run over to Isaac's house if I have a problem."

"Oh." Kaylee had a guess as to Nick's real objection to the living arrangements. "Is the cabin very near Isaac's house?"

Felicia nodded. "Closer than it seems because of all the trees, but it's on the Pine family land. I'd never be able to afford to stay on the island if Isaac wasn't letting me stay in the cabin for free."

Again, Kaylee could see why Nick had a problem with the cabin. "Rentals can be high here in the summer." She felt like her reply was a little inane, but she didn't want to get in the middle of trouble between Nick and his new girlfriend.

When they got close to the water, Felicia stopped suddenly and Kaylee paused beside her, eliciting a disgruntled sigh from Bear. He loved meeting the ferry and wasn't pleased about the wait.

"Do you think there will be a lot of people on the afternoon ferry?" Felicia asked.

"I don't know." Kaylee shrugged. "Most of the day visitors come in on the morning ferry, so maybe not."

Felicia's gaze turned again to the bustling area around the ferry landing, and Kaylee realized the woman was frightened. She wondered if Felicia might have some kind of social anxiety problem. Or was there a more specific reason for her fear?

Giving herself a mental shake, Kaylee tamped down her curiosity. She had to stop letting her imagination run away with her. *There isn't a mystery behind every bush.*

4

Spotting the Learners on Location students was easy, as the teens came ashore in a flurry of chatter and pointing. It seemed they all wanted to see everything the island had to offer, all at once. Behind the ten or so students, two adults followed, looking only slightly overwhelmed.

Kaylee hurried over to meet the group. "Are you guys our Learners on Location?"

The youths responded loudly and together. "Yes!"

A woman who appeared to be only a few years past her own teens managed to push through the clump, popping out in front of Kaylee. "Hi," she said brightly, sticking out a hand to shake. "I'm Jenna Olsen. William and I are handling the Learners on Location."

Kaylee shook her hand, marveling at the energy radiating from the woman. The combination of excitement and cheer reminded her a bit of Bear. As if sensing a kindred spirit, Bear wagged his tail furiously and barked, adding to the noise around him.

"Is that your dog?" one of the teen girls asked Kaylee as she dropped to her knees next to Bear and held out a hand for him to sniff.

"Seems likely," another girl drawled, shifting her graffiti-print backpack on her shoulder. "Considering she's holding the leash and all."

The kneeling girl made a face at the other before returning to rubbing Bear's ears. "He's adorable."

"He knows it too," Kaylee said with a grin. "I'm Kaylee Bleu. I'll be leading one of the learning experiences you'll have while you're on Orcas Island. For today, I just wanted to welcome everyone and make sure you're settled."

The teens seemed to remember their manners and a chorus of thanks rang out.

Jenna reached into the clump of teens and pulled the other adult leader forward, introducing him as William Tomlinson. The man seemed an exact opposite of Jenna, quiet and glum where she was cheerful and talkative. "William is in charge of frowning," Jenna stage-whispered to Kaylee, which made the tall, dark-haired man blush.

The man cleared his throat and quickly introduced each of the teens. He rattled them off so fast that Kaylee knew she'd need to hear them more than once before she'd have the teenagers sorted out in her head.

The girl who'd been petting Bear popped up. "Are you two sisters?" she asked, gesturing past Kaylee to Felicia.

Felicia laughed lightly and Kaylee introduced her. "We're not sisters, just new friends." At the word 'friends' she saw Felicia's face brighten even more. Kaylee felt a pang of concern. Was Felicia lonely on the island? She made a note to encourage the Petal Pushers to reach out and include Felicia in the group.

"That's amazing," Jenna said. "You two look so much alike."

Kaylee didn't know what to say to that. She honestly couldn't see much resemblance. *Sure, Felicia and I both have long, straight, dark hair, but is that such a unique feature that it makes everyone comment on it?*

"Do you both live here on Orcas Island?" William asked, drawing Kaylee's attention from her musings.

"We do," Felicia said. "Kaylee even has a business here."

"That's right. We're eager to visit The Flower Patch," Jenna said, then she turned to the teens. "Aren't we?" There was a general murmur of agreement, though it definitely sounded more enthusiastic from some of the kids than others.

"Will you be telling us something of the botanical origins of the plants?" one of the boys asked, pushing a pair of wire-rimmed glasses up on his nose as he spoke. Kaylee struggled to recall his name for a moment, then remembered that it was Carter. "I'm very interested in botany."

"Really?" Kaylee said, trying to keep a triumphant tone out of her voice. She made a mental note to tell Luke. "I'm a plant taxonomist by training. The creative side is a newer passion."

The teen girl who'd made the snarky remark about Bear spoke up again. "I'm sure all the science stuff is fascinating, but I'm more interested in flower arranging as an art."

"And I'm sure the demonstration will include that, Pepper," Jenna said, giving the teenager a mildly disapproving look.

"Do you do flower arranging too?" Pepper asked Felicia.

When Felicia didn't answer, Kaylee turned to look at her, then frowned in concern when she saw how pale her new friend had become. Felicia stared at the rest of the ferry crowd, and she clearly hadn't heard the girl's question.

"Felicia?" Kaylee reached out to touch the other woman's arm.

Felicia jumped and spun to face Kaylee, wide-eyed. "What?"

"Are you all right?" Kaylee asked.

"I'm fine. I have to go, though. I just remembered an appointment." She aimed a brittle smile at the teens. "It was nice to meet all of you. Maybe I'll see you at The Flower Patch tomorrow." Then she spun and hurried away, vanishing into the bustle around the docks.

"She's jumpy," Pepper said.

William cleared his throat, drawing attention away from Felicia's departure. "I'll go collect the bus. Then we can head out to the campground."

"Can we stop for snacks on the way?" one of the boys asked. Kaylee searched her memory for his name, but it didn't come to mind.

"We'll see," William said, then he turned sharply and headed back toward the ferry to collect the vehicle.

"It was so nice of you to come out and meet us," Jenna chirped at Kaylee. "Everyone we've dealt with for this program has just been darling."

"I'm glad to hear it," Kaylee said. "We're always happy for the chance to show off the things we love doing."

They chatted a bit longer, and Kaylee made an effort to ask each of the teens at least one question so she could get a better sense of their personalities. As soon as William arrived with the large van that served as the group bus, the teens hurried off. Jenna offered one more effusive thanks before following the students.

Kaylee watched the group for a moment, thinking about how much fun they were going to have, then spoke to Bear at her feet. "I guess it's time to go back to work."

Bear wagged his tail in response and they returned to the shop. When Kaylee pushed open the door, she was surprised to find Nick standing at the counter chatting with Mary.

"And here she is," Mary said as Kaylee walked in.

Bear immediately spotted Nick and danced around his feet until the deputy knelt to pet him.

"Were you wanting to talk to me?" Kaylee asked.

"You sound surprised." Nick gave her a teasing grin. "It's always a pleasure to talk with you, Kaylee."

"I don't know about that," she said. "I can remember a few times where you weren't at all happy to talk to me. So what brings you here today? Are you shopping for flowers?"

"I am," Nick told her. "I want something really special for Felicia. It's our one-month dating anniversary, and I want to show her that I appreciate that." Then he smiled a bit sheepishly. "Plus, she's a little mad at me, and I hoped to smooth it over with flowers."

Kaylee managed to keep the pleasant expression on her face even while she did the math. If this was Nick and Felicia's one-month anniversary, then she was already dating Nick when she went on Roz's whale watch, the whale watch where Felicia and Isaac Pine had been too wrapped up in one another to pay attention to the whales. Granted, all that was just gossip from Roz, who was prone to blowing things out of proportion.

"Hello?" Nick said. "Earth to Kaylee."

Kaylee pushed down her concerns and smiled. "Sorry about that. I just saw Felicia, by the way. She walked down to greet the Learners on Location kids with me."

Nick's grin widened. "I'm going out to the campground to give those kids a lesson in identifying animal tracks and tracking tomorrow morning."

Kaylee made a face. "Tomorrow? Thanks, Nick. My flower arranging lesson is going to seem pretty dull after that. How can a florist compare to the excitement of learning how to track wildlife from a sheriff's deputy?"

"I don't know about that," Nick said. "You've had some pretty exciting happenings here at the flower shop."

"I really don't think some of those incidents would be proper topics to share with teenagers," Mary said. "And speaking of happenings, I was just telling Nick that you had a scare on your way in this morning."

Kaylee felt her face grow warm. "Oh, I'm sure that was nothing."

"It sounded like something," Nick said. "Someone ran you off the road?"

"Not really. I had actually already moved off the road, but there wasn't much shoulder at the spot, and I ended up tumbling into the undergrowth." She sighed. "It really wasn't anything worthy of police involvement. It's not like we don't know that summer can be open season on wild driving."

"Just because we know it's going to happen doesn't mean we shouldn't pay attention to it," Nick said. "Did you get the car's plate number? Or see the driver? I wouldn't mind tracking the person down and having a stern word."

"It all happened so fast," Kaylee said. "And it was in the hilly part of the drive from the cottage, so the car was there and then it was gone. About all I can say is that it was a blue sedan."

Nick gave a dry laugh. "Not exactly a rare color. Still, I'll keep an eye out. Though maybe almost hitting you put enough fear into the driver to keep it from happening again."

"I hope so."

"So," Nick said, "tell me about the Learners on Location kids. Did they seem happy to be here?"

Kaylee brightened. "They did. They're a boisterous bunch. I don't envy the adults in charge of them. Teens can be challenging. They're old enough to think they can take care of themselves, and young enough to be impulsive. Granted, I met their leaders and at least the lady, Jenna Olsen, has every bit as much energy as the kids."

"She'll probably need it," Nick said.

At that, the shop door opened again, and Bear left Nick's side to give his usual welcome bark for the new arrival. An older man held the door for the woman with him. Bear's tail wagged rapidly, but then he seemed to look past the two coming through the door.

He dashed for the door in a small brown blur, scooting between the couple coming in.

"Bear!" Kaylee cried, shocked by the little dog's actions. Bear never ran off like that.

The dachshund seemed not to hear her. He raced across the porch, barking rapidly.

Kaylee dodged the newcomers and slipped out the door, still

calling for Bear. She'd barely stepped onto the porch when she heard a loud screech of brakes and the blare of a horn.

Her stomach plummeted.

"Bear!"

5

In her state of alarm, it took Kaylee a moment to realize Bear was still on the porch, though he stood at the very edge of the top step, barking wildly. She snatched him up before he could run down the stairs.

Nick had followed Kaylee out of the shop. "What's going on?" he asked, then bolted past Kaylee, nearly leaping off the porch. "Felicia!"

Felicia stood at the edge of the street, surrounded by people. She held her hand to her chest, staring down the street with round, frightened eyes. Nick pushed through the small group. "Felicia, what happened?"

A portly man in a T-shirt printed with whales answered for her. "Some idiot nearly ran her over."

"What?" Nick yelped.

"It's nothing," Felicia said, laying a hand on Nick's arm. Her voice trembled despite her words. "I should have paid more attention when I started to cross the street, that's all."

"More attention?" The portly man was indignant. "You were at the crosswalk and it was clear. It's not like you were darting into traffic. That idiot in the blue car came out of nowhere."

Kaylee had started toward the shop door with Bear, but she froze at the man's words. *Blue car?* Could it have been the same blue car that had run her off the road? What were the odds of that?

"Could you ID the car?" Nick asked the man.

The witness seemed to deflate a bit. "Sorry, I didn't see it all that well. It was definitely blue though. Maybe a rental?"

"It was a sedan," another man called out. "I couldn't tell you the model though."

While they talked, Felicia detached from the group and joined Kaylee on the porch. She reached toward Bear, still nestled in Kaylee's arms, and stroked his ears. "Bear's barking was what made me stop," she said in quiet voice. "I might have been all the way into the street if not for him. I don't think I could have gotten out from in front of the car in time if I'd taken another step."

Bear bathed Felicia's cheek in doggy kisses.

Nick finished quizzing witnesses and joined them. When he heard about Bear's role in saving Felicia, he praised the dog enthusiastically. Kaylee thought her pup might burst from happiness.

"Nick," Kaylee said hesitantly. "You know about the car that nearly hit me this morning. It was a blue sedan too. I'm sure that's a coincidence, but I wanted to mention it."

Nick turned away from Bear and raised both eyebrows. "Things that seem to be coincidental often aren't. I don't like having two such similar incidents so close together."

"Thankfully no one was hurt either time," Kaylee said. Nick frowned and nodded toward the bandage on Kaylee's arm, so she amended her comment. "Thankfully no one was hurt badly."

"You think it was the same car?" Felicia asked.

"I don't know." Kaylee glanced around at the handful of vehicles parked along the street. "Blue isn't exactly a rare color for a car, and I didn't see the one that nearly hit you. I just wanted to mention the similarity in case this guy continues driving crazy around the island." She waved a hand to take in the bustle along the sidewalk. "This isn't exactly a lonely stretch of road where you might feel safe speeding."

Nick's frown grew even darker. "No it isn't."

"Maybe it wasn't an accident."

Nick and Kaylee turned to meet the watery blue eyes of an

elderly woman with a puff of white hair around a tiny wrinkled face. Kaylee had seen her in the group surrounding Felicia after the accident and vaguely recognized her, so she was probably one of the regular summer visitors. "Why do you say that?" Kaylee asked. "Did you see something?"

She shook her head, making her white puff bounce. "Nope. But I can see you two ladies resemble each other pretty strongly. Maybe we have a serial killer on the island targeting pretty women with long, dark hair."

Nick groaned. "I'm sure we do not have a serial killer on Orcas Island. This isn't a big city."

The woman sniffed. "I don't see any reason why you'd think serial killers just live in the city. I've read true crime books. Serial killers *like* rural areas."

"But I doubt they like islands. Clean getaways are kind of hard here," Nick said. "And you might consider changing your reading choices."

The woman glared at him. "You best respect your elders, young man." Then she clutched her shopping bag—which Kaylee noticed was from Between the Lines—to her chest and walked off in a huff.

"Oh, Nick," Felicia scolded. "You could have at least acted like you were considering her idea."

"Really?" Nick flicked his gaze from Felicia to Kaylee. "Do you two think someone is targeting you because of how you look?"

Felicia didn't answer, though her expression changed from near amusement to concern.

"I'm sure it's a coincidence," Kaylee said to soothe the tension. "Traffic does get more challenging in the summer."

Nick put his hands on his hips and gave her a stern glare. "With that in mind, you should probably stay off the bike for a little while. I'll see if I can find the owner of the blue car. Even if it's just a run-of-the-mill crazy driver, I'll feel better if you're not out there endangering yourself."

"Riding my bike isn't endangering myself," Kaylee said, beginning to feel slightly annoyed. "I'm not going to miss out on perfect biking weather just because someone is a bad driver. I'll simply be more careful." Despite her strong words, she suspected she was only reacting to being told what to do—she wasn't exactly eager to go biking after this.

"And I was being a bit careless," Felicia said. "I'll make an effort to do less woolgathering at crosswalks. I'm sure it'll be fine."

"I'll assume this means neither of you wants to file an official report," Nick said, sounding annoyed.

Felicia's expression morphed into one of horror. "Definitely not."

"I didn't see enough for a report to be worthwhile," Kaylee admitted.

Nick huffed out a frustrated breath. "Fine. I know better than to try to talk either of you into anything." He turned to Felicia. "Can I buy you a coffee, at least?" He nodded toward Death by Chocolate.

"Does she have tea?" Felicia asked as she gave Bear one last pat on the head. "I might like soothing over stimulating right now."

"She has a nice selection of teas," Kaylee answered. "I recommend the chamomile blend."

"Thanks, Kaylee." Felicia smiled and slipped her arm through Nick's.

Kaylee watched as Nick and Felicia walked on to the bakery. She gave Bear a last little hug. "You did a good deed, but don't run off again. You nearly gave me a heart attack." Bear licked the end of her nose and Kaylee giggled. "Flirt."

On Tuesday morning, Kaylee set her alarm to get up early so she'd have time for her normal morning routine plus some flower cutting. With the warm sunny days and plenty of gentle showers, Wildflower Cottage had lived up to its name in abundance. Kaylee intended to bring a nice selection for the teens to use in their arrangements.

Bear trotted along at her heels as she walked around the yard. She cut the *Daucus carota* that she'd been planning on, then added some *Lathyrus odoratus*. The range of pastel colors in the sweet peas would be perfect for anyone in the group that wanted to avoid some of the more dramatic colors of many of the shop's blooms, and Kaylee loved their sweet, delicate scent. Though many considered sweet peas to be wildflowers, Kaylee knew they weren't really native to Orcas Island. The flower had actually come originally from the Aegean Sea region and had been refined by a Scottish gardener named Henry Eckford in the late 1800s and early 1900s.

She snipped stems until her bucket was completely full, then carried it to her car. Bear's tail began to wag furiously as soon as Kaylee had the bucket loaded. She gave him a smile. "You seem to be ready for work."

After settling Bear in the car, Kaylee headed out. This was her first drive down the road since the accident the morning before. Instead of biking home, she'd even given in and let Mary drive her back to Wildflower Cottage the previous night. "But we're going to get back in the saddle," she told Bear. She knew she couldn't let too many days pile up before confronting a fear, but one day didn't feel like enough.

She had the windows down to enjoy the warm breeze, which meant she heard the deep roar of an engine. "Someone's coming up fast," she muttered, feeling her stomach clench. Was she going to experience a repeat of the morning before?

Then she realized the sound of the motor wasn't coming from behind her. A convertible crested the hill ahead and came into view, then passed in a flash. Kaylee let out a breath that she hadn't realized she was holding. The car that drove by wasn't blue and wasn't a sedan. Though it passed faster than she would have preferred, the low-slung silver sports car gave her plenty of room. She'd even recognized the driver as Isaac Pine.

"Wow," Kaylee said aloud. "The summer people sure are early risers this year."

Because it was moving so fast, the convertible was soon out of sight of her rearview mirror. Kaylee wondered briefly if Isaac lived somewhere near her. He couldn't be a close neighbor, as she'd met all of those.

When the view of the ocean opened up on one side of the road, Kaylee felt the last of her nervous energy dissipate. The morning before had simply been a fluke. She spent the rest of the ride singing cheerfully to Bear, who howled in response. She wasn't sure if the howling was his effort to join in the songs or merely critiques of her singing, but she found that the activity chased any lingering worries away. She arrived at The Flower Patch with her usual bright cheer.

As she walked into the shop, Mary offered her a cup of coffee. "Jess brought over one for each of us," she said. "Along with a bucket of flowers that I put in the cooler."

Kaylee held up her own bucket. "Will there be room for mine?"

"Just barely."

They walked back to the coolers with Bear trailing along behind them, his nails clicking on the floor. Kaylee spotted the new bucket of flowers right away. "Oh, look at the *Delphinium elatum*. I love that shade of blue. It would be a wonderful contrast with the pinks of some of these sweet peas."

While they shifted containers to make a spot for Kaylee's

flowers, they chatted about the few morning orders that would need to be filled before the teens arrived. When they heard the front door opening, Mary hopped up to greet the newcomer.

Taking a fortifying sip of coffee, Kaylee smiled as she saw that their customer was the slender, young man who hadn't missed a day the shop was open since he and his wife had come to the island. Kaylee wished he'd bring his wife in sometime so she could see the woman who inspired such devotion. With a smile, Kaylee got to work on their list of orders.

As always, the task of choosing flowers and turning them into art gave Kaylee a sense of contentment, making the passing of time feel like water flowing unnoticed around her. She jumped at a tap on her arm. "The kids are here," Mary said.

"Perfect timing." Kaylee held up the small arrangement of lilies and carnations she'd been working on. "I just finished the last order."

Mary took it from her to put it in the holding cooler, and Kaylee hurried out of the workroom to find the teens near the front counter. Several were kneeling on the floor, petting Bear, who soaked up the attention like a furry sponge. Others walked around, peering at things in the shop. Exuding a slightly stressed air, the two adult chaperones watched them all.

"Welcome to The Flower Patch," Kaylee called out, drawing their attention. "I hope you enjoyed your first night of camping."

One of the boys slouched next to the counter. He bobbed his head. "It was cool. I think I heard a bear."

"You probably heard a raccoon," William corrected. "They're noisy and, since not everyone followed the food rules, we definitely had one visiting last night."

"Ugh, rules," another boy complained. "We're supposed to be on vacation."

"The rules are designed to keep you safe," William said.

"And I'm sure they know that," Jenna added, her voice perky. "It was just a single mistake."

"A mistake that brought a bear," one of the girls said.

"Raccoon," William said firmly.

Pepper stood up from where she'd been petting Bear and rubbed her hands on her long shorts. From her ears dangled long, silver earrings, the same ones she'd worn the day before when they got off the ferry. Kaylee noticed she also wore the same narrow leather bracelet around her wrist. The teenager certainly had her own sense of style.

"The only good thing I can say about tent life," Pepper said, "is that at least our campsite is the closest one to the bathroom. It's bad enough to walk to the bathroom in the dark without turning it into a hike."

"You wouldn't have to walk or hike if you restricted liquids in the evening," Carter told her, "instead of guzzling soda."

"I had to have something to help get those burned hot dogs down." Pepper looked askance at William.

William seemed to puff up slightly. "Fine. Tonight everyone can handle roasting their own hot dog."

Pepper rolled her eyes. "Lucky us. More hot dogs."

Kaylee had stood smiling through the whole exchange. She suspected the two adults were earning every dollar they were being paid to chaperone this group. At least she hoped they were being paid. "Well," she said, changing the subject to get the group moving. "I have lots of flowers for your arrangements today, so let's get started."

"Back here," Mary sang out from the work area.

The teens trooped in that direction and Bear followed. Kaylee started after them, but she stopped when Jenna caught her arm.

"Can I leave the kids with you for a little while?" the chaperone asked. "William and I want to run next door and get some treats for everyone."

"Of course," Kaylee said, though she suspected the two adults were mainly motivated by a desperate need for coffee after a long night at the campsite.

As Jenna and William left, Kaylee took a quick glance out the front windows. She remembered Felicia's remarks about attending the Learners on Location demonstration. Had she forgotten the time or found something more interesting to do? Kaylee wished she had Felicia's number so she could call her.

For a moment she thought about contacting Nick to ask about Felicia, then shook her head. "If she wanted to be here, I'm sure she'd be here." And with that, she headed back to the work area, thoughts of her new friend fading as the opening lines she'd planned for her presentation began running through her head.

She was surprised to find all the teens were attentive as she talked. She began with the history of flower arranging. She'd known that might be a risk since she didn't know if teens would be interested, but she liked the idea of letting the kids know they were taking part in an actual art form that was immensely old.

"We know the ancient Egyptians made highly stylized arrangements," Kaylee said. "Their carved stone reliefs and ancient paintings show arranged flowers."

"Well," one grinning boy said, "they had to give flowers to their mummies too." He laughed while all the other teens groaned.

Kaylee bit back a giggle, then finished up her introduction and pointed to the variety of small vases, jars, and other vessels in the middle of the table. "Almost any container can work for a floral arrangement, but the type you choose will affect your design." She held up a mug with a grinning cat face on it in one hand and a simple but elegant vase in her other hand. "A whimsical choice tends to work best with a whimsical design, while this vase requires something more sophisticated. So, let's begin by choosing the container that you think best matches your personality."

One of the girls held out her hand. "I'd like the cat mug, please. I'm definitely a crazy cat lady in training."

Though some decisions took longer than others, each teen seemed eager to talk about why they'd made their individual choice. And the enthusiasm continued as they picked flowers and shapes for the arrangements. Kaylee explained about focal points and composition, and the kids took what she said and ran with it.

More than once, Kaylee wondered about Jenna and William. They certainly seemed to be taking advantage of their break from chaperone duties. She didn't really need their help so she didn't mind, but it did seem odd that they would leave their charges for so long.

As Kaylee watched the teens work, she quickly picked out the few who had a really good eye for design. She wasn't surprised to see that Pepper had the most unique arrangement by far, and the one that had the best composition. "Mixing the elegance of roses with the sweetness of daisies was an effective choice," she told the girl.

Pepper beamed at her. "I can't take credit. I was inspired." Then she lifted her leg to table height, showing off a pair of combat boots printed in a floral pattern of roses and daisies.

Kaylee laughed, wondering how she hadn't noticed the boots earlier. "You definitely have your own style. But aren't those boots hot in the summer?"

Pepper shrugged. "It's worth it, and the shorts mean I don't sweat to death. These boots are my favorite because I can have flowers wherever I go."

One of the teen boys hooted. "Don't believe her. She likes them because she can kick harder with them on."

Pepper smirked at him. "That is a bonus."

Before the discussion of kicking could go any further, the talk was interrupted by Jenna staggering in with a tray loaded down with drinks. Plastic bags hung from her arms. "Come and get it!" she chirped.

The teens abandoned their arrangements to grab beverages and peer into bags.

"I thought William was going to help," Kaylee said.

For the first time, Jenna's expression lost its brightness. She scowled and whispered fiercely, "That's what I thought, until he said he had to use the restroom. I think he's still hiding in there. Talk about using any excuse to avoid being a pack mule. He was almost that bad yesterday when it came time to set up camp. I think he's just lazy."

"Is he still in the bathroom at the bakery?" Kaylee asked.

"As far as I know."

"Maybe he's ill. Did you knock on the door at least?"

Jenna looked scandalized. "Of the men's room?"

Carter spoke up from nearby. "I could go in and check on him. Or at least knock on the door." He didn't roll his eyes, but Kaylee thought the tone in his voice implied an eye roll at Jenna's concern over knocking on a men's room door.

"Maybe we should go check on him." Kaylee turned briefly back toward the table. "The kids are mostly done with their arrangements and they don't need me to finish up." She called out to Mary, who stood on the other side of the room. "Do you mind if I step next door?"

"Go ahead," Mary said. "I can hold down the fort."

Kaylee and Carter started toward the door, only to notice Jenna wasn't following. "Aren't you coming?"

The young woman was sipping from a tall cup. After a long guzzle, she sighed deeply. "I suppose. Though I expect he'll be along now that he doesn't have to carry anything."

They walked over to Death by Chocolate and were greeted by Jessica. "Back already?" she said as they walked in.

"Apparently we lost someone," Kaylee said. "William came in but never came out."

"He's in the bathroom," Jenna said, making it sound like a criticism.

"Oh." Jessica reached below the counter and came up with a key, which she gave to Carter.

The group filed to the restroom door near the back of the customer area. Carter knocked and received no response. He pounded harder, making the door rattle a bit. Still nothing.

"I think I should probably go in." Carter glanced at Kaylee, Jessica, and Jenna, who were all standing back, out of the line of sight of the bathroom. He unlocked the door and nudged it part of the way open.

With a shout, he stumbled backward, almost falling, then faced the adults, his eyes wide.

The women surged toward the door as Carter pushed it the rest of the way open. The bathroom was bright, clean, and airy. It was also occupied.

William lay sprawled and unmoving on the floor.

6

Kaylee's hand rose to her mouth as the shock of the scene froze her, but then she followed Jessica into the restroom. Carter dropped to his knees beside William, grabbing the man's wrist to check for a pulse. At the same moment, William moved, turning his head toward Carter and opening his eyes.

"What happened?" William asked.

"That's what we wanted to know," Carter said. "What are you doing on the floor?"

Kaylee and Jessica joined Carter to help William sit up. The group leader raised a hand to his head. "I'm a little dizzy." He gave them all a thin smile. "I shouldn't have skipped breakfast. My blood sugar must have crashed."

"Are you diabetic?" Jessica asked.

"No," William said. "I have just been so busy, and I didn't eat much last night. Even though the hot dogs I cooked were fine. Then I skipped breakfast this morning. I probably just need something to eat."

"Do you think you can stand?" Jessica asked.

"Yeah." William started to shift position, and the others moved to help haul him to his feet. That was when Kaylee noticed Jenna still standing in the bathroom doorway. She didn't seem concerned about William. If anything, her expression was annoyed.

Jessica kept hold of William's elbow. "Come on out to the front, and I'll get you something to eat. I have some savory scones. That might be a better choice than the doughnuts your coworker bought. You don't want your sugar to rise too fast."

"Yeah," William said. "That might be good."

There wasn't room for all of them to get through the bathroom doorway at once, so Kaylee stayed back. Her gaze drifted to the sink, and she frowned. *What is that?* She stepped closer to peer at the sparkling white porcelain. The edge of the sink was smeared with what appeared to be soil. Bits of green were caught in the dirt, and more plant matter had fallen into the basin. There wasn't a lot of it, but why was there any? Kaylee knew that Jessica kept the bathroom very clean, so why would there be dirt and plant matter in the sink?

She examined the space above the sink. Though most restrooms had mirrors over the sink, this one had a window, and a mirror was mounted closer to the door. The window was open, and a faint breeze blew in, carrying the scent of salt water. Kaylee supposed it wasn't really odd that someone would open a window in a bathroom, but she wondered if the open window was somehow related to the mess in the sink. *Would someone throw dirt in through the window? And if someone did, why?*

"Kaylee?" Jenna had walked into the bathroom.

Kaylee turned away from the window. "Is William going to the clinic?"

Jenna rolled her eyes. "No. I don't think there's anything wrong with him. You wouldn't know it to look at him, but I think he might be a bit of a drama queen. And he didn't help at all yesterday. I have no idea why he volunteered with Learners on Location. He couldn't possibly be less interested in the kids."

"Maybe he was already feeling unwell," Kaylee suggested. She was uncomfortable gossiping about a man they'd just found sprawled unconscious on the floor.

"Maybe." Jenna shrugged, then she took a deep breath and smiled, though it was only a faint replica of the enthusiastic expression she'd worn the day before, or even that morning. "I'm not usually this quick to judgment. You're right. I should be more understanding." She bobbed her head as if convincing herself of what she'd just said. "Your friend is feeding him. He might be a changed guy after a little food."

Kaylee smiled along with her. "Maybe so. We'd best get back to the kids. I'm sure they're all done with their arrangements by now."

Jenna's smile loosened to something more natural. "They've probably plowed through the food too. Maybe I should pick up something for myself. I like the sound of the savory scones."

"I'm sure they're delicious," Kaylee said. "Everything here is amazing." She followed the other woman out, casting one last glance toward the sink and the mystery of the dirt and plants.

They found William seated at a table, sipping from a steaming cup and eating a scone. Jenna walked to the display case and peered in. Jessica smiled at her, then she slipped over to Kaylee. "Weird," she whispered. Then she pointed to Oliver, who, Kaylee thought, actually did seem a little droopier than he had earlier.

"Would you do me a favor?" Kaylee asked.

"Sure."

Kaylee quietly explained about the soil and plant matter in the sink. "I didn't want to take a sample in front of anyone." She tilted her head toward Jenna. "After we leave, could you collect some for me? I know it's silly, but this has been so strange. I just feel like I ought to keep a sample."

"Hey, you know me," Jessica said, her eyes sparkling. "I love weird. I'll drop it off later."

"No rush."

Jenna called out to Jessica then, so Kaylee's friend hurried over. Kaylee walked to the small table where Carter sat near William.

"Are you sure you don't want to see a doctor?" she asked William.

The chaperone smiled sheepishly. "No, I feel fine now. Really, we need to get back to the kids." His eyes widened. "They aren't all alone at the floral shop, are they?"

"No, Mary is with them," Kaylee said.

His smile twitched. "Of course. Yes. Nice lady. Still, we should get going." He raised his voice to call out to Jenna. "I'm going to head back to the kids. You come when you're ready."

Jenna nodded, her expression blank. "I'll be right there."

Kaylee followed William and Carter out of the bakery. She had expected the Learners on Location program to be fun and interesting, but the behavior of the two adults running it was turning out to be one of the most notable parts so far.

As soon as they got to The Flower Patch, the teens rushed up to William. "Did you really lock yourself in the bathroom to keep from having to carry stuff?" Pepper asked.

William looked shocked. "Of course not. Why would you say that?"

Kaylee clapped her hands to interrupt any remark that might serve to feed the clear rift between the adult leaders of the program. "Did everyone finish their arrangement?"

Her question completely shifted the teens' focus, and each of them wanted her to admire their work. And she did admire it. The arrangements weren't exactly professional, but several designs showed out-of-the-box thinking that Kaylee appreciated. She made a mental note to push the boundaries more when she thought up new bouquets for the shop. "You have all impressed me this morning," she told the group, smiling. "Your creativity is truly inspiring."

After the delighted teens left with their flowers, the shop seemed almost too quiet. Kaylee began cleaning up the area where the teens had worked. Mary helped between customers. Bear ran between greeting new visitors and watching Kaylee clean up. Eventually, the back-and-forth finally wore him out and he flopped down on the floor, resting his head on his short front legs, and fell asleep. He was still napping when Kaylee swept the last of the dropped greenery into a dustpan.

Mary walked over with the bin where they put leftover plant bits for composting. "I hope we're still on for this afternoon."

For a moment, Kaylee had no idea what Mary was talking about, but then it flooded back. It was Tuesday. She'd promised to go with Mary to the funeral home. Kaylee winced inwardly, but she managed a cheerful voice as she said, "Of course we're still on."

"Great. I know it's not the most pleasant thing to ask of you."

"I've asked unpleasant things of you," Kaylee said airily. "I'm glad to do anything that helps you feel better."

Mary reached out and squeezed Kaylee's arm. "This will. It really will."

When Mary showed Kaylee the lunch she'd packed to share as a gesture of gratitude, Kaylee felt positively guilty for the reluctance she still felt. She hated the idea of her friend dying someday and certainly didn't want to help pick out a casket for her, but every time she felt a kind of internal flinching at the idea, she reminded herself of what a good friend Mary had been to her and her grandmother before her.

Still, when the time finally came to close up the shop early for the appointment, Kaylee worked hard not to show the nerves she was feeling. "I think Bear will be okay here alone," Kaylee said hesitantly. "He doesn't tend to tear things up, and none of the plants he could reach would hurt him if he decided to be a rascal and take a nibble."

"You know," Mary said thoughtfully, "we could do a presentation about that topic at the library sometime."

Kaylee blinked at her. "What topic?"

"Pets and plants," Mary said. "People don't always realize

how dangerous houseplants and floral arrangements can be if dogs and cats chew them up. Just last week, you talked Geoffrey Pratt out of that bouquet for his wife because of their cats."

Kaylee nodded. "Judy told me her cats were plant chewers, and Geoffrey was going to bring home lilies. They can cause organ failure in cats."

"See?" Mary said. "That's information our clients could use."

"Maybe we could make a poster. Or flyers. Then we could share the information all year."

Mary rushed over to the counter to make a note. "That's a great idea." When she finished writing, she squared her shoulders. "We'd better get going. I don't want to be late for my appointment."

I wouldn't mind, Kaylee thought, but she followed her friend out of the shop.

The Akin Funeral Chapel was a small funeral home on Sea Cliff Avenue. The building was pale stone with a sharply peaked roof and arched windows. Giles Akin was the town's elected coroner, so Kaylee had talked with him a number of times since moving to Turtle Cove, usually in connection with police investigations. As she had been in Seattle, Kaylee was often called on by the Orcas Island sheriff's department to identify plant material found at crime scenes.

Thelma Akin met them at the door of the funeral home. The curvy, auburn-haired woman's smile was warm, if slightly harried. From behind her, Kaylee caught the scent of lavender. She'd smelled that at the funeral home in the past and wondered if the soothing smell of the essential oil was Thelma's touch. She backed up slightly to let Mary in ahead of her. She'd let Mary handle this, and she'd just be there for moral support when she was called upon.

Thelma led them into the building and apologized. "I'm afraid Giles won't be able to meet with you. He wasn't feeling well this morning, and I made him stay home in bed since he only had one appointment today. He told me you wanted to see our selection of caskets. I can help with that."

"I hope it's nothing serious," Kaylee said, momentarily forgetting her decision to be a silent supporter. She hated to think Giles might be seriously ill.

"I'm fairly certain it's a cold," Thelma said as they paused just inside the doors. "But I find it best to rest at the first sign of sickness and give your body a chance to fight off the germs. It was hard to explain this reasoning to Giles, though, as he'd run himself into the ground given the opportunity."

Mary laughed. "I nearly have to sit on Herb to get him to rest when he gets a cold or the flu."

Thelma started down a hallway lined with framed peaceful landscapes. "Our display room is this way."

"I know it must seem strange, my wanting to pick out a casket when I'm perfectly healthy," Mary said.

"Not strange at all," Thelma said over her shoulder. "I think it shows wise planning."

Mary brightened some at that. "I remember Giles saying something about planning back when he was preparing for the funeral of a retired accountant. The man had created a folder with all the plans for his service and burial."

Thelma nodded. "That happens more than you'd think. People like lifting that burden from their loved ones. No one wants to make decisions like that when they're grieving."

"Giles told me he wished everyone did that," Mary said. "I want to be that thorough."

"Then you're in exactly the right place." Thelma swept a hand toward a large doorway. "This is our display room. Don't hesitate to ask any questions, and feel free to touch linings if you want. I'm here to help."

Kaylee resisted the urge to hang back in the doorway and made herself follow along close to Mary. Her friend stopped in front of one pale casket. "I like the color of this one," she said. "But why is it closed?"

Thelma frowned at the casket. "We keep all of these displays propped open so you can see the interior. I have no idea why this one is closed."

"Maybe someone spilled something into it?" Kaylee asked.

Thelma was clearly scandalized at the idea. "We don't allow food and drinks back here." She reached for the edge of the lid. "And this is really a lovely option."

She swung open the lid and shrieked, jumping back away from the casket and letting the top slam down. Though the lid had only been partly open for a moment, it was long enough for Kaylee and Mary to see what was inside.

A body lay in what should have been an empty casket.

The body of Felicia Lewis.

7

Kaylee stood against the wall of the display room watching Sheriff Eddie Maddox talk to Mary. The tall sheriff's solemn expression was mirrored in Mary's own. Since Mary had once been a dispatcher for the sheriff's department, Kaylee suspected they'd take anything she said with special seriousness.

Kaylee fussed with the hem of her light summer sweater, nervous fingers folding the loose knit into pleats then smoothing them out again. She couldn't believe what she'd seen. Why would anyone do that? Why kill someone and then leave the person in a casket? She blinked her stinging eyes. She'd liked Felicia. They could probably have become real friends, but now she'd never know her.

Kaylee's gaze shifted closer to the casket, where Deputy Robyn Garcia talked to Thelma. Kaylee knew it would be her turn to answer questions soon enough. She doubted it would take long, as she couldn't offer much.

Suddenly she heard the sound of running footsteps in the hall, and then Nick burst through the door. He shoved past Alan Brooks, the youngest deputy in the department, whose job at that particular crime scene seemed to be keeping anyone from doing precisely what Nick had just done.

"Where is she?" Nick demanded.

Both the sheriff and Deputy Garcia abandoned their questioning to stand in Nick's way. "You know you shouldn't be here," the sheriff said, his tone kind but firm. "We'll have questions for you, but you can't be on the case."

"Questions for me?" Nick gave the sheriff a blank expression for a long moment, then realization dawned. "Like I'm a suspect?"

"You were dating the victim," the sheriff said, his voice still patient. "You know procedure. We are going to have to follow it to the letter with this one. We can't afford any sign of impropriety in this investigation considering one of my deputies is closely associated with the victim."

Nick winced. "Can we not call her 'the victim'? Her name is Felicia."

The sheriff gripped the younger man's shoulder in a fatherly gesture. "All right." He switched back to official investigation mode. "Garcia, you can finish up with Thelma and talk to Kaylee."

The deputy bobbed her head, sending her light brown ponytail swinging, and walked back to Thelma.

The sheriff held up his notebook and focused on Nick. "Do you know of anyone who might want to hurt Felicia?"

Nick shook his head slowly. The gravity of the situation seemed to be sinking in. He clearly had to force himself to focus on the question at hand. "Isaac Pine has been hanging around her a lot, but he's never shown any sign of being violent or even angry. Well, not angry with her." His expression darkened. "But he did hang around way too much."

"We'll talk to him," the sheriff said. "When did you last see the vic—Felicia?"

"Yesterday afternoon," Nick said. His voice sounded far away, as if he were remembering someone else's life. "We had coffee together during my break at Death by Chocolate. I didn't talk with her after that. I had a ton of paperwork to catch up on."

"And after work?"

"I went home," Nick said numbly. "Alone. Didn't see anyone. Didn't talk to anyone."

"Thanks." The sheriff snapped his notebook closed. "We'll keep you updated, but I want to be clear: You don't go anywhere near this case. No investigating on your own, no going through case files, no questioning other deputies or anyone you think is involved."

"Sheriff," Nick said plaintively. "I have to help."

"Then call me if you think of anything. Otherwise, let us do the job. I'm not kidding, Durham. Any defense attorney worth half his schooling would use your involvement to cost us a conviction when we catch whoever did this. And we will catch him. Or her. The best thing you can do for your girl is keep your nose out of it and let us know if you think of anything that might be helpful."

The sheriff glanced away from Nick and pointed at Kaylee. "Stick around. We'll be with you in a minute." He gestured to Deputy Brooks. "Start collecting fingerprints before we get any more folks wandering around the crime scene." The sheriff walked back to Mary, and his voice dropped too low for Kaylee to eavesdrop.

Kaylee left her spot by the wall to join Nick. "I'm so sorry," she murmured.

His gaze was locked on the casket, where Deputy Brooks was dusting for fingerprints. "She's special—was special," Nick said softly. "I feel like I've known her forever instead of a month." Then he sighed and crossed his arms over his chest. "But maybe I didn't know her at all. I could tell she had secrets, but I thought we had time for her to learn to trust me with them."

Nick's reference to his time with Felicia brought the memory of Roz Corzo's remarks back to Kaylee. She made a mental note to talk to Roz about exactly how "sweet and cozy" Isaac and Felicia had been. Then she looked into Nick's troubled brown eyes. Did he know Felicia had still been seeing Isaac? Was her friend in a lot worse trouble than a broken heart?

The sheriff joined them and clapped a hand on Nick's shoulder. "You need to go home. I'll come by when we're all done here. I might have more questions. But for now, you need to go, Nick."

For a moment, Kaylee thought Nick might argue with his boss, but finally his posture wilted slightly. He simply nodded and left.

Mary approached Kaylee and squeezed her arm. "I'll go on to the shop now," she said. "I'm sure Bear is wondering where we went."

Kaylee's eyes widened. She'd forgotten all about Bear at the shop alone. "Thank you. I'm sure he could use a walk."

"He'll get that, and maybe a little snack." Mary smiled kindly. "I'll double-check things at the shop and bring Bear to the Petal Pushers meeting with me."

"Thank you. Bear will like that."

After Mary left, Kaylee found herself looking into the shrewd, dark-brown eyes of the Orcas Island sheriff. Eddie Maddox had a strong chin and high cheekbones, the latter likely from his Alaskan Native mother. The combination gave him a strong, almost fierce demeanor. Kaylee liked the sheriff. He was calm, smart, and generally no-nonsense, with a good, kind heart. As worried as she was about Nick, she knew they could trust the sheriff to do the right thing.

Kaylee managed a weak smile. "I thought Deputy Garcia was going to interview me."

"I changed my mind," the sheriff said plainly. "How well did you know the victim?"

"Not as well as I would have liked. I had just met her, but I was sure we were going to be friends," Kaylee said sadly. She explained about meeting Felicia at dinner just days before and then chatting with her when they went to meet the ferry. "There was one incident you might want to know about."

The sheriff raised thick eyebrows. "Oh?"

"A car nearly hit Felicia yesterday. She insisted she was being careless, but the odd thing is that I'd nearly been hit by a car with the same description only that morning." She elaborated, telling the sheriff all she knew about each incident.

"That could be a coincidence," the sheriff said. "Bad driving isn't exactly rare this time of year, but it does bear further investigation."

After a pause, Kaylee decided to tell the sheriff about Felicia's peculiar behavior at the ferry as well. "I didn't think a lot about it at the time, but in retrospect, I think Felicia was frightened of someone or something. She was definitely jumpy."

"I appreciate all these details," the sheriff said. "But keep in mind that nearly anything can feel ominous after something like this. Much of it has no bearing on the case at all. I don't want you worrying about it."

"I'm not worried, but I am concerned. I liked Felicia, and Nick is my friend."

"And mine as well, but I have to do my job." Maddox's gaze became piercing. "What did you think about Nick and Felicia's relationship?"

"They were obviously very fond of one another."

"Did you ever see them fight or argue?" he asked. "Any conflict at all?"

"Well, I only met her a couple days ago," Kaylee said, hedging slightly, since she hated to say anything that might make Nick look bad. She could tell by the expression on the sheriff's face that she didn't fool him. "I do think there were hard feelings between Nick and Isaac Pine."

"Mary said they had an altercation at O'Brien's," the sheriff said.

Of course—Mary saw it all too. Kaylee realized it was silly of her to think the sheriff wouldn't hear about every aspect of Nick and Felicia's relationship. Turtle Cove was like any other small town, where everyone seemed to know everyone else's business. On a good day, it made the community feel warm and caring.

On a bad day, it felt a lot like idle and occasionally malicious gossip. "Isaac Pine came to the restaurant, clearly intending to talk to Felicia. He seemed to have something important to say to her or talk about."

"And Nick didn't like that."

"I think Nick saw it as aggressive," Kaylee answered. "I thought it was more urgent than aggressive, but I could understand Nick's reaction. He wasn't angry at all with Felicia, though."

"But she wasn't pleased by his actions, even though he meant them as protective?"

"I think she might have been embarrassed," Kaylee said. "It was a public place. I suspect she would have rather just heard Isaac out and left more quietly. I got the feeling that Felicia was shy, or at least uneasy in public places."

"Did you get any indication that Isaac Pine might intend to hurt Felicia?"

"Not at the restaurant," Kaylee said. "I don't actually know the man. I've only seen him twice."

"Twice?"

Kaylee explained about Isaac buzzing by her on the highway. "He was driving a bit fast for the conditions, but he gave me plenty of room in the pass. I think I was just unnerved by it because of my near miss the day before, with the blue sedan I told you about."

"And Pine wasn't driving a blue sedan?" the sheriff asked.

"Not when I saw him on the road. He was in a convertible."

The sheriff closed his notebook, but his eyes stayed on Kaylee. "We're going to have to tread carefully with this investigation. The Pines are a family of wealth and influence, and we can't appear to be trying to turn suspicion away from Nick onto Pine."

Kaylee wasn't sure why the sheriff was telling her this, so she didn't know how to reply. She quietly said, "I see."

"I doubt it, but let me be plain. Nick must stay completely out of this investigation. In fact, I'm going to recommend he take advantage of some of the vacation time he has built up. That way, I don't have to do anything official to keep him out of the investigation."

Kaylee winced. She doubted that was going to sit well with Nick. "I hope you can talk him into it."

"I can be very persuasive, but that's only the tip of the problem." He ran a hand through his thick, black hair, which was peppered with gray. "You are a good friend of Nick's, and he has to be on our suspect list. That means we're not going to be asking you to examine any evidence in this particular case."

"That's understandable." Kaylee rather doubted there would be any plant-based evidence anyway. Felicia hadn't been found in the woods, and the showroom at the funeral home was immaculately clean.

"It isn't that we don't have full confidence in you," the sheriff added. "You know that."

"I do. I understand why you can't bring me in. Are we done here?"

"For now. I may contact you later if I have more questions."

"I'm not hard to find." She could see smears of fingerprint powder on the casket's shiny surface, but thankfully she couldn't see Felicia inside. "I hope you find out who did this soon."

"We'll do our best. Thank you for your time." The sheriff started across the room to where Thelma stood near the doorway, one arm crossed over her middle and one hand resting on her cheek. "I hope Giles is on his way," the sheriff said. "We need a coroner."

Thelma dropped her hand. "I called, and I sent Jay over to help him get going. He may be a little dopey from cold medicine, but Jay will make sure his dad gets here."

"As long as he doesn't sneeze on anything," the sheriff said. He gave Kaylee a pointed look. "Thanks again. You have a good evening."

Kaylee didn't think there was much chance of that, but she gave the sheriff a tight smile and a nod. She would be glad to get out of the funeral home. Even with the soothing scent of lavender in the air, she felt wound tight from stress. She knew Nick didn't have anything to do with Felicia's death. At least she thought she knew it. She wondered what it meant psychologically for the killer to leave Felicia in a casket, if anything. Was it a sign of care and concern? In that case, she would consider Isaac a good suspect. But it might also be some kind of flaunting, perhaps related to Felicia's nervous reaction to the ferry and the crowd. Was she afraid of someone? If so, it certainly appeared that she'd had good reason for it.

Kaylee stepped out the front door of the funeral parlor. The sun was low in the sky, suggesting more time had passed than she'd thought. She wondered if she was already late for the Petal Pushers meeting. She stood near the double doors and fished in her purse for her phone, intending to check the time. As she searched the purse, she edged away from the doors and near a tall planting to the side in case anyone needed to come out. She didn't want to be plowed into.

She'd just gotten her fingers around her phone when a hand reached out from the shrubbery and grabbed her. With a yelp, she was hauled into the bushes.

8

Before Kaylee could shriek out the fear building in her throat, she heard a voice she recognized, even at a whisper. "Don't yell," Nick said.

Kaylee squirmed around until she was facing him, then smacked his arm. "You scared me half to death," she hissed.

"Sorry." He didn't look sorry, only intense, and even a little wild. "I needed to talk to you privately, and no one inside can see me out here."

The space behind the tall plantings was too tight for Kaylee to back up much, but she leaned away and crossed her arms over her chest. She was still shaken from the scare. "Fine. Talk."

"I want you to help me find out who killed Felicia."

She gaped at him. "That's a job for the sheriff's department."

"I *am* the sheriff's department," he insisted. "Or part of it. This is more my job than anyone's."

"I was in there. I heard the sheriff. You're supposed to stay completely out of this."

"And that's why I need your help," he said.

"No way. The sheriff told me to stay out of it too."

"And you always stay out of investigations when you're asked," he said drily, and Kaylee winced. He did have a point. In fact, it was a bit ironic that Nick was now asking her to get more involved with a case, since he was usually the one telling her to stay out of trouble.

"I don't know, Nick," she said, though she knew her tone wasn't exactly firm. She remembered the sheriff's words, but it was hard to say no to the raw grief in her friend's eyes.

"Kaylee, I liked Felicia," he said. "With time, I think I could have more than liked her. I can't just sit on my hands while other people investigate. I have to know who did this. I owe it to her."

Kaylee shifted uncomfortably. She never wanted to get on the wrong side of the sheriff, and he'd been plain about Nick and Kaylee's involvement. At the same time, she couldn't count the number of times Nick had helped her out. "What do you want me to do?" she asked tentatively.

A grin of relief flashed over Nick's face. "First, I want you to tell me everything. Every detail of what you told the sheriff, of what you saw in"—his voice hitched slightly—"in the casket."

"I'm not sure this is the best spot for a long conversation," Kaylee said. "Eventually people will be coming out of the funeral home, and I think they'll wonder about the talking bushes."

"Yeah, fine, you're right. Are you heading home? I could meet you there."

"I wasn't going home. I have a Petal Pushers meeting," Kaylee said. "And they'll wonder where I am. In fact, I'm sure they're already wondering where I am. And it's not impossible that Mary might call the sheriff if I don't head over there."

"Yeah, I can see that. But I need to talk to you, Kaylee. You notice things. I want to know what those things were."

"And I'll be happy to tell you." In fact, the request sounded a lot easier than anything she might have thought he'd ask. "I just can't do it right now."

Nick ran a hand through his hair in frustration. "I hate to risk you forgetting any details. It's best to get this while it's fresh."

"I'm on my way to the Petal Pushers meeting," she said. "There is zero chance they aren't going to want to hear all about whatever I know. I'm not likely to have a chance to forget it."

"Fine, but as soon as you can, write down as much as you

can remember. It'll help keep it fresh. And I'll come by your house tonight after the meeting."

She shook her head. "No you won't. I've had a pretty horrific day, and I'm going to go home and sleep. You can come by in the morning if you don't mind getting up early. I'll put the coffee on, and we can talk then."

It was obvious Nick hated the idea of waiting that long, but finally he gave in. "I have a few things I can check into tonight. I'll see you in the morning." He named a time, and Kaylee agreed. Then she pushed her way out of the bushes, relieved to find no one around to see her acting so strangely, and headed for her car.

As soon as Kaylee entered the Old Cape Lighthouse keeper's quarters, she was greeted with a mixture of relief and avid curiosity by the rest of the group. Clearly happy to see her, Bear added his barks to the buzz of questions, making it impossible for Kaylee to pick out and understand anything.

The Petal Pushers garden club had four regular members, though sometimes other gardeners around Turtle Cove would come to meetings if the group was planning a community-wide event. Tonight, however, was just the core four: Kaylee, Mary, Jessica, and DeeDee. DeeDee owned a mystery bookshop called Between the Lines, so she definitely wouldn't be able to resist the mystery of Felicia's death.

Kaylee held up both hands and her friends backed off enough to give her some breathing room, everyone falling silent as they waited to hear what Kaylee had to say. "I'm sorry I'm late. I'm sure Mary has pretty much told you everything there is to tell."

"Except why Sheriff Maddox kept you so long," Mary said.

"I guess he wanted to hear it all again," Kaylee said, feeling a pang of guilt for not telling her friends about her talk with Nick. She was relieved to be able to switch to something completely truthful. "The sheriff said I won't be helping the department with this case. My friendship with Nick means I'm too close to it."

DeeDee picked up a brownie from the table, drawing Kaylee's attention to the snacks. Her stomach growled at the sight. It had been hours since she'd eaten.

DeeDee must have heard it because she grinned and held out the treat. "You sound like you need this more than me."

"Thanks," Kaylee said. She accepted the brownie and took a bite of chocolaty goodness.

"I can't believe I didn't know about any of this until Mary and Jessica filled me in tonight," DeeDee said. "A fight at O'Brien's. Someone trying to run Kaylee down. And now a murder."

"No one tried to run me down," Kaylee said, hoping that was the truth. "It was just a crazy driver."

"I rather doubt that." DeeDee began counting off incidents on her fingers as she named them. "Someone tries to run you down. Then someone tries to run Felicia down. Then someone murders Felicia and leaves her at Akin Funeral Chapel. When you factor in the strong resemblance between you and Felicia as reported by people who have seen you together, it's a definite pattern."

Kaylee really didn't want to entertain that particular theory. It sounded silly. She certainly *hoped* it was silly. She turned pointedly to Mary. "The sheriff certainly talked to you a long time."

Mary looked unhappy, but she nodded. "I felt terrible, but I had to tell Sheriff Maddox about the incident at the restaurant. It certainly didn't seem like Isaac was okay with losing his girlfriend to Nick."

Kaylee sighed. "I'm not entirely sure he'd lost her." She tapped a finger on her chin. "Jess, do you remember what Roz told us about her whale watch?"

"Sure. Why?"

"That whale watch took place about two weeks ago, give or take," Kaylee said. "But Nick says that he had been dating Felicia for a month. She was seeing Nick when she went on that whale watch."

"The whale watch where Felicia and Isaac Pine were so wrapped up in each other they barely reacted to the whales," Jessica said, her eyes widening.

"You know what I think?" DeeDee asked. "I think you need to talk to Roz again. Find out more details about the interaction with Isaac and Felicia. Maybe she misinterpreted it. Maybe they had their heads together because he was blackmailing her or cooking up a scam."

"Or planning a heist," Jessica added eagerly.

"Planning a heist?" Mary said. "You don't think that might be a tiny bit dramatic?"

Jessica shrugged and picked up a brownie. "What could possibly be more dramatic than what the killer did with Felicia's body?"

The other three women shuddered in unison.

Kaylee walked over and sat down on one of the chairs arranged for the group's meeting. It felt like she'd been living the longest day she could remember.

Mary followed and sat beside her. She patted Kaylee's hand lightly. "I'm so sorry."

"Sorry for what?" Kaylee asked in surprise as Jessica and DeeDee joined them.

"For making you go with me to the funeral home," Mary said. "I know you didn't really want to go. Who would? And if I hadn't dragged you along, you wouldn't have had to see that."

"But then you would have had to deal with it alone. And you didn't make me or drag me." Kaylee smiled at Mary. "I wanted to do whatever it took to give you peace of mind."

Mary leaned back in her chair with a sigh. "It certainly didn't go as planned. That poor girl. She was so sweet every time I saw her. Who would want to hurt someone like that?"

"I think we should learn more about Isaac Pine," DeeDee said. "He sounds like a suspect."

"I think he is probably at the top of the sheriff's list," Kaylee said. "Unfortunately, Nick has to be on that list too."

"Loved ones always are," Mary said. "Love goes wrong too often for the sheriff to strike Nick off the list just because he's a deputy."

"Nick is another reason we should learn more about Isaac Pine," DeeDee said. "I like Nick, and he's always so good with Polly and Zoe. He really listens to them and treats them like equals. There aren't many adults who do that."

"I think we can all agree that Nick didn't do it, and he certainly deserves to be cleared," Mary said. "But I don't think that means Isaac Pine definitely did."

"He did seem rather intense at the restaurant," Jessica said hesitantly.

Kaylee had to agree with that. Both Isaac and Nick had been intense that night. And Kaylee had seen Isaac racing down the road just that morning, as if he had somewhere to be in a hurry—or somewhere to be gone from. Maybe there was a good reason for him to be at the top of the sheriff's suspect list. Then she thought of Felicia's behavior at the dock. "I think Felicia was afraid," she said quietly. "Or at least nervous about something. But at the restaurant, she didn't act like she was afraid of Isaac."

"I don't understand," Jessica said. "What was she afraid of, if not Isaac?"

Kaylee told her friends about Felicia's nervous behavior when they walked together to meet the Learners on Location kids. "She seemed to be watching for someone."

"Still could have been Isaac," Jessica said. "Not that I'm in a hurry to see Isaac Pine in trouble either. He's been in the bakery a few times and he's very nice. Reserved, but polite."

"That doesn't necessarily mean anything," Mary said. "People aren't always their true selves in public."

There was a moment of silence as the women digested this.

"Not to change the subject, but totally changing the subject," DeeDee cut in, "you mentioned meeting the Learners on Location group at the ferry. I know you had them at The Flower Patch this morning. How did that go? I'm leading a little writing workshop with them at the bookstore, and I want to know what to expect."

Relieved to turn the conversation away from murder, Kaylee said, "A writing workshop? I didn't know you were a writer."

DeeDee gave them a sheepish grin. "I'm not really, but I have a writing section at the bookstore, so I had plenty of advice at my fingertips. Though I came up with my writing prompts totally on my own based on Turtle Cove. Now, tell me. How terrified should I be of these teens?"

"Not terrified at all," Kaylee said as Mary nodded in agreement beside her. "I thought they were wonderful. They really are very bright and interested in trying new things." She hesitated, then added, "Their leaders can be a bit weird though."

"How so?" DeeDee asked.

"They don't seem thrilled to be working together," Jessica offered. "They were in the shop this morning. Jenna is massively cheerful, though she was clearly very annoyed with William about something. And William is stiff." Her eyes twinkled. "He even fainted stiffly."

"Fainted!" DeeDee put a hand to her cheek. "I've missed everything."

Kaylee was happy when Jessica took over the narration about the fainting and recovery of William Tomlinson. She sat back and ate the rest of her brownie, her musings only interrupted when Bear stood on his hind legs and braced himself against her knees, begging to be picked up. She scooped him up and settled him on her lap, still thinking about the Learners on Location leader on the floor of the restroom. Her train of thought meandered to the soil and plants she'd found in the sink. In the more alarming events of the afternoon, she'd forgotten about them. She turned to Jessica. "Jess, do you have the sample from the sink?"

"I sure do," Jessica said. She hopped up to dig in her purse and returned to hand Kaylee a small plastic bag with bits of soil and plant matter in it. "I took some photos too, before I cleaned all the mess out of the sink and off the floor."

"There was some on the floor too?" Kaylee asked.

"Yes, though that probably came from William's shoes. They are staying at a campground, so I imagine they're tracking up floors wherever they go."

Floors, sure, Kaylee thought, *but sinks?*

She slipped the bag into her purse, then sat petting Bear as the conversation morphed from the Learners on Location to a summer gardening project DeeDee's daughters were doing. "It's a pizza garden. They're growing all kinds of herbs and toppings," she explained. "And they insist on doing everything themselves. As soon as the tomatoes ripen, they plan to have a pizza party. I saw you all on the guest list that Zoe is keeping."

"Sounds great," Kaylee said. She loved the bright, inquisitive girls.

When the meeting finally wound down, Kaylee was glad to be heading home. Bear had clearly had all the excitement he could handle for one day as well, since he snoozed noisily in the back seat. Kaylee smiled at him in the dark, impressed as always by how much sound could come from one little dog.

The night was clear, and they were only a few days from

a full moon, which helped light the dark road near Wildflower Cottage. Though she couldn't see all her plants in the dark, Kaylee could smell the lavender through the window. Unfortunately, the aroma reminded her of the scent at the funeral home, which brought a stark memory of Felicia's pale face in the casket.

Kaylee shut off the car and rubbed the goose bumps on her bare arms. She hoped she'd eventually be able to cut off that unfortunate association in her head. "Lavender is part of Wildflower Cottage," she said softly as she opened the car door. "And I love it here."

Her quiet whisper and the interior lights of the car were enough to wake Bear, and he sat up, tail wagging. "Yeah," Kaylee said. "I'm glad to be home too."

She carried Bear as she approached the white farmhouse. She knew any bad feelings would soon be eclipsed by all the good memories she had of the wonderful farmhouse and the grandparents she adored who'd lived in it for so long. Coming home was like being greeted by all her most joyful childhood memories.

Then she saw a shadow move on the porch of the cottage, and Bear began barking wildly. Someone was on the porch in the dark, waiting for her.

9

Even before she could see the intruder clearly, Kaylee could tell Bear's barks weren't anxious. The little dog clearly recognized whoever waited on the porch and was happy to see their guest.

The shadowy visitor came to the porch steps and the light of the moon illuminated him. "I thought that meeting would never end," Nick said.

Kaylee set Bear down so he could bound over to greet his friend, and Nick knelt to give the dog a good petting.

"Is scaring me half to death a new thing with you?" Kaylee demanded as soon as she felt calm enough to speak. "I thought we were meeting tomorrow. In fact, I seem to remember insisting on it."

Nick shrugged as he stood back up. "I couldn't wait." He peered out across her yard and into the darkness beyond. "I have to do something."

"It's a bit late to be doing much tonight, but you can come in for a cup of tea if you want."

Nick raised his eyebrows. "Tea?"

"You don't need any coffee," she said sharply. "And I know I don't. Come on in." She led him into the farmhouse, turning on lights as they passed through to the kitchen. Her nerves were soothed by the familiar surroundings. As she filled the kettle under the tap, she asked, "Is this going to be the new normal for us? Meeting clandestinely?"

Nick paced the kitchen. "It wouldn't take Sheriff Maddox long to figure out that I'm not staying away from the case if we're seen together in public."

"That sounds a little paranoid. We run into each other in public all the time."

"And when we do, we'll act normally."

Kaylee had trouble equating the intense man watching her fix tea with the easygoing flirt she'd known all this time. She waved him toward a chair. "We might as well sit down while you tell me what you want me to do. I assume you have a plan."

He dragged a chair back from the table and sat in it. Bear ran over and sat up with his front paws on Nick's leg. Nick rubbed the dog's ears absently. "I think the first thing you need to do is talk to Isaac."

Kaylee blinked at him. "I don't even know the man. Why would he talk to me?"

"Because everyone talks to you. It's that sweet, innocent look you have. You don't come off threatening, and he doesn't have any reason to dislike you." He held his hands out. "I can't talk to him. He kind of hates me. And he'd call the sheriff the second I showed up."

"He doesn't have any reason to trust me." She turned away to pour the water into the mugs. "And I don't think my looks are quite as magical as you suggest. If I appear innocent at all, it probably comes from the fact that I normally try to *be* innocent of wrongdoing, like interfering in a police investigation with you."

"Finding out who killed Felicia isn't wrongdoing," Nick argued.

Kaylee carried the mugs to the table. "Don't you trust the sheriff to do his job?"

"Come on, Kaylee. I'd rather not beg for your help, but I'm not above it."

To give herself a moment to think, she grabbed a jar of honey and a couple of spoons, then sighed and joined Nick at the table. "Fine. Do you have his phone number?"

Relief swept away the darkness on Nick's face, and he pulled out his phone. "I do. You call, and I'll walk you through what to say. Arrange a meeting. I think you'll be able to read the man better face-to-face."

Kaylee held up a hand. "I'll call him, but not tonight. If I'm going to be meeting with someone you suspect might be a killer, I'd prefer to do it in broad daylight. Tomorrow is soon enough."

"Meeting him tonight would make it easier for me to get close to you both without being seen."

"Then you'll just have to work at it," she said. "No night meetings with potential killers. I can't believe I even have to argue this. What happened to the Nick Durham who is constantly scolding me for not being more careful?"

Nick sat back in his chair and stared into his mug. "You're right. I'm sorry. I won't let anything happen to you, Kaylee. Call Isaac tomorrow, when you're ready. Then let me know the second you have a time set for the meeting."

"That's one thing I can promise," Kaylee said. "You'll be the first person I call."

She tried to make small talk after that, but it was clear to her that he couldn't focus, and he left a little while later, having barely touched his tea. Kaylee washed his mug, then carried the rest of her own tea to her bedroom. She needed something to take her mind off the horrors of the day, and she was pretty sure the novel she'd been reading would fit the bill.

Soon she was snuggled in her bed with Bear beside her, a book in her hands, and the mug within reach on the nightstand. Though she felt more secure at home, she found the upset of the day wasn't easy to banish. And she knew it shouldn't be. A woman had died, and Kaylee couldn't stop seeing her still face in the casket. Though she knew the sheriff wouldn't be pleased if he ever found out, she was glad to be helping Nick track down the killer. Felicia deserved the full effort of everyone who had known her.

Finally, she sighed and shut the book, choosing instead to think about the day ahead. She wondered what kind of man Isaac Pine would be. He'd been upset the one time she'd really seen him, and she couldn't imagine he'd be any more laid-back after hearing of Felicia's death. She switched off the light and pulled Bear close for a snuggle. The dachshund grumbled sleepily at being disturbed.

"Tomorrow might be a tough one," she whispered to him.

Bear gave her a small comforting lick on the chin.

Wednesday morning brought rain, and Kaylee was a little grateful for it, because it meant she couldn't possibly ride her bicycle to work. Since she intended to call Isaac and arrange a meeting, riding would have been out of the question anyway, but Kaylee couldn't banish her feeling that she needed to get back on the bike before her nerves grew into a full-blown phobia.

"I don't need any more internal conflicts," she told Bear as she carried him to the car, holding an umbrella over the two of them.

To her surprise, the rain had passed by the time she reached the flower shop, and Kaylee found someone waiting to speak with her. Pepper sat in one of the rockers on the wide porch of The Flower Patch. She hopped to her feet the second she saw Kaylee and Bear. Once she was standing, however, she seemed at a loss for words and simply fidgeted with the narrow leather bracelet on her arm. Kaylee set Bear down on the porch, and he rushed over to prance around the teen's feet.

"How nice to see you, Pepper," Kaylee said in greeting. "Is the rest of your group here?"

Pepper reached down to give Bear a quick pat then stood

back up, shaking her head and making her earrings swing. "I told Jenna that I had to talk to you."

Kaylee paused. "Okay. Do you want to talk out here or inside?"

Pepper shifted her weight again. "Here's fine. I was wondering, though . . ." She took a deep breath and blurted, "Could I help out at the flower shop? I could sweep or dust or—just anything really. I love the flowers. I'd like to be around while you work on them."

"I wouldn't want to get in the way of the other programs," Kaylee said. "There are several wonderful presentations planned for all of you."

"I know, and I appreciate it. I don't want to miss any classes. But there's also sightseeing and hiking. I'm not really into that. I could use that time to be here. If that's okay with you."

"That would be fine with me, but you'll have to get permission from Jenna and William. I don't want to create problems for the program."

Pepper rolled her eyes. "Like they'd care."

"What do you mean?" Kaylee asked, concern blooming in her mind.

Pepper hunched her shoulders. "Nothing. I'll go ask them."

She raced from the porch as though someone was chasing her, and Kaylee had to stifle a laugh. "It must be nice to have that much energy," she told Bear.

She found Mary waiting on a customer as she walked in. It was the young man who had come in every morning to buy a flower for his wife during their stay. Today, he was holding a pink-and-white stargazer lily. "Nice choice," Kaylee said as she set Bear on the floor.

"My wife loves pink," he said.

"Will you be on the island much longer?" Kaylee asked.

His smile became teasing. "Are you afraid you'll run out of flower varieties for me?"

"Not a chance," Mary chimed in. "We're fully stocked at the moment."

"I knew you wouldn't let me down." He nodded to each of them and headed out the front door. Kaylee looked after him, wondering why he'd avoided the question about how long they'd be staying.

As if reading her mind, Mary said, "Maybe they haven't decided how long they'll stay. Orcas Island can be captivating."

"I certainly think so."

Mary leaned across the counter, examining Kaylee closely. "Did you sleep okay last night?"

Kaylee reached up to touch her face. Did her restless night show? "I'm fine. Yesterday was tough."

"I'm sure we'll all feel better when the sheriff finds Felicia's killer." Mary gestured toward one of the shop windows. "I saw Pepper chatting with you. She wouldn't tell me what she wanted. Is she okay?"

"She was asking for a job, or at least a chance to hang out here." Kaylee smiled. "I think we may have a floral designer in the making."

"A budding florist?" Mary asked with a wide grin.

Kaylee groaned at her.

While she worked on the day's orders, Kaylee rehearsed her call to Isaac in her head. Finally, she pulled out her phone and leaned against the long worktable, her back to the door. *Let's get this over with.*

As soon as Isaac picked up, Kaylee introduced herself. "I knew Felicia," Kaylee said. "Not as well as I would have liked, but I think we were getting to be friends."

"She mentioned you," he said. "She was looking forward to seeing some sort of demonstration at your shop."

Kaylee winced at that. She'd noticed Felicia was missing

during the program. If she'd raised an alarm then, would it have made any difference? Would Felicia still be alive? "I wonder if I could meet you somewhere to chat a bit about her. I know it probably sounds crazy, but I feel a little guilty."

"Guilty?"

She explained about Felicia missing the program. "I wish I'd called someone about it. I didn't have Felicia's phone number, and I just let it go. I wish I hadn't."

"I'm sure there's nothing for you to feel guilty about, Miss Bleu. But if you'd like to talk about Felicia, I'd be glad to. Too many people feel like they can't talk about someone after they die, but Felicia deserves to be remembered."

"Thank you," Kaylee said. "Do you want to meet here in town? Or should I come to you? I'm flexible." She held her breath, hoping he'd offer to come to the shop. She'd feel much safer meeting him in town with all the bustle of shop customers.

"If you don't mind, I would appreciate it if you came here," he said. "I don't think I have the emotional fortitude to leave my house today." He explained how to reach his property and Kaylee realized he didn't live all that far from her own cottage, though he was a bit farther inland. She thanked him for making time for her and hung up.

"Wow." At the sound of Pepper's voice, Kaylee spun to find the girl standing a few feet away. "I heard someone say that you solve crimes. Is that what you're doing? Trying to find out about the murder?"

"You know about the murder?" Kaylee asked.

Pepper gave her the look perfected by teenagers everywhere, the one that suggested adults were slow-witted. "It's all anyone is talking about."

"Well, I'm no detective. And I would really prefer not to talk about any of this right now."

"Sure," Pepper said with no hint of remorse in her voice. She continued to watch Kaylee with an eagerness that was slightly disconcerting.

Kaylee tried to think of something to distract the teen from the topic of murder. She gestured toward the bracelet Pepper had been fiddling with earlier. "You have unique taste in jewelry. Big flashy earrings and a simple leather bracelet."

Pepper held up her wrist. "My grandfather made this for me. He made one for all of his grandchildren from a pair of chaps he had. He was a trick rider for the movies when he was young."

"That must have been interesting."

Pepper grinned. "I come from an interesting family."

"I don't doubt that. How about you help me with some floral arrangements for the shop?" Kaylee asked, happy to have drawn the teen's attention to something other than homicide. "We like to have some available for customers who pop in to grab and go."

Enthusiasm brightened Pepper's face even more. "Really? Do I get to handle the flowers?"

"It would be hard to make an arrangement any other way." As Kaylee walked Pepper over to the coolers, she explained a little about how to design a cost-effective bouquet. "You want to choose your flowers so that you get the most from your design without letting the cost rise too high."

"So, cool and amazing on a budget," Pepper said. "I have a lot of experience with that."

Kaylee laughed. "Then you'll be a natural at this." She gestured toward one section that still held a few of the flowers left over from the Learners on Location demonstration. "These flowers were all donated, so I'd love for none of them to go to waste if possible. Anything you make with these flowers can be used in an inexpensive gift option. And I'll give you a percentage of every arrangement that sells. Does that sound like a deal?"

"Wow, thanks. I'll use the donated flowers," Pepper said. "That way if no one wants my stuff, you won't be out any money."

"I don't think we have to worry about that," Kaylee said, remembering the stunning arrangement the girl had created the previous morning.

As they worked together on a few small arrangements, Kaylee was glad that Pepper showed no more interest in the murder. She certainly didn't want to do anything that might endanger the teen. Of course, she'd like to avoid doing anything that might endanger herself either. *I'm sure I'll be fine.* But she found she didn't really believe it. Not at all.

10

Kaylee went up to the second-floor office and closed the door to call Nick, thinking it was the best place in the Victorian to avoid being overheard. She felt a little foolish being so secretive. Part of her wanted to tell Mary that she was helping Nick, but since Mary had worked with the sheriff for years as a dispatcher, Kaylee suspected her friend's loyalties might be torn. It was best not to put Mary in that position at all.

"When are you meeting Isaac?" Nick asked without preamble when he picked up.

She told him, then said, "None of this is making me very comfortable."

"I know. And I appreciate what you're doing more than you could know. I promise you won't have to keep my secrets long."

"Exactly how close will you be during my meeting?" Kaylee asked. "Because I really don't want to get in the middle of an altercation between the two of you."

"Since you're meeting him during the day, it'll be hard for me to be as close as I'd like, but I have a work-around. When you get to Pine's house, call me, then leave the line open and put the phone in your purse. I should be able to hear your conversation. Then if there's any trouble, I'll come running."

The idea of trouble knotted Kaylee's stomach, but she agreed. After finishing the call, Kaylee returned to the sales floor and found a customer at the front counter. It was the romantic young man who bought flowers for his wife daily. "Coming back for a second flower?" she asked him as she approached.

"My wife is allergic to lilies," he said. "I can't believe I forgot. I gave the flower to one of the housekeepers at the inn." He held up a spike of pale purple flowers with white centers, one of Jessica's donations for the flower-arranging course. "She'll like this more. I can't believe something this beautiful could be so inexpensive."

"*Delphinium consolida*," Kaylee said. "I should plant some at my cottage. I've needed something with a nice spike like that." She smiled up at the man. "Larkspur is in the same family as buttercups."

"I'll tell my wife," he said with a smile that reached up to his brown eyes. "She's been learning a lot about flowers since our wedding."

"Does she garden?" Kaylee asked.

His smile faded a little. "We live in an apartment in the city. We don't have the space."

"A person can do amazing things with container gardening, if you have a good light source," Kaylee said. "We have a book on it."

The young man happily added the book to his purchases and left the shop humming.

"Do you have another copy of that book?" Pepper asked. "We don't have room for a garden at our place either."

Kaylee smiled at the teen. "Of course. In fact, the book is our gift to you for helping out this morning."

Pepper opened her eyes wide. "Whoa, thanks."

Swirling thoughts about Felicia's murder and her pending meeting with Isaac kept Kaylee unusually quiet as she finished up the orders they had, pausing only to comment occasionally on the work Pepper was doing nearby on the worktable. She would need to leave soon if she was going to meet Isaac at the designated time, and that meant she was going to have to come up with an excuse. Sighing at the dilemma, she looked up and noticed Mary standing behind the counter, shooting her a worried glance.

"This one's done," Pepper said, pulling Kaylee's attention

back. "Should I go put it in the front cooler?"

Kaylee nodded absently. As soon as Pepper bounced out of the area, Mary came in. She hesitated for a moment, then said, "I wanted to tell you that you won't have to go casket shopping with me anymore."

"Have you changed your mind about planning your funeral?"

"Not at all. Herb felt guilty about my running across a dead body when he wasn't there." Mary smiled a little. "Though I don't know what he thought he could have done about it. Anyway, he said he realized he should have been there. So next week, I'll be going back with Herb."

"I would have gone with you," Kaylee said softly.

"I know." Mary gave her hand a friendly squeeze. "You're a great deal like your grandmother, you know that?"

"That is a high compliment." *And one I don't deserve.* Kaylee couldn't imagine her beloved grandmother sneaking around and potentially undermining a police investigation. Bea Lyons was a forthright person.

"Are you all right?" Mary asked. "I know you liked Felicia. This all seems to have hit you very hard."

"I'm fine." Kaylee hoped the smile she offered appeared more authentic than it felt.

Apparently it didn't, as Mary said, "I think you could use a break. Why don't you take Bear for a walk around, maybe to the park? That always cheers you up. Pepper and I will handle things here while you're gone."

It was just like her to be so kind, and Kaylee thought warmly that Mary was the one who was like Bea. "You're so sweet," she said. "I think I'll take you up on that offer. In fact, I have an errand I need to run." She backed up to speak to Bear under the table. "Want to go for a ride?"

Bear leaped to his feet. He was always up for a ride.

Kaylee was relieved when Mary didn't ask any details about Kaylee's errand. *At least I didn't have to lie.* Keeping something so big from Mary still felt deceptive, but Kaylee pressed back her well of guilt as she snapped on Bear's leash.

She risked being late by darting into Death by Chocolate for some of Jessica's unbeatable salted caramel chocolate cookies. Somehow the treats made the prospect of questioning a grieving man to see if he might actually be a killer less daunting.

While driving out to the property, Kaylee felt nerves knotting her stomach. When the Pine mansion finally came into view, Kaylee actually gasped. She was fairly certain that both The Flower Patch and Wildflower Cottage would fit inside the huge, showy estate. The Georgian style of the building made it seem very much out of place on Orcas Island. "And this is their summer place," she said to Bear. "I can't imagine what their main house must be like."

Kaylee made the call to Nick. When he answered, she confirmed where she was, slipped the phone into her purse, and hopped out of her car. She was lifting Bear out when Isaac emerged from the front door of the imposing house. "Kaylee?"

"That's me," Kaylee said. "And this is Bear."

Isaac laughed lightly. "That's the tiniest bear I've ever seen."

"But he has a big heart."

The man held out a hand to Bear. Bear took one sniff and then ran his head under Isaac's hand. Isaac laughed again, clearly charmed. "What a great dog."

"Thank you," Kaylee said. "I happen to agree." While Isaac continued petting Bear, Kaylee saw that his smile was contrasted by dark circles under his blue eyes. Immediately her heart lurched. "I'm so sorry for your loss." Remembering the goodies she'd brought, she retrieved them from her car. "I brought cookies from the bakery in town. They always make me feel better."

The smile slipped from his face and the stark grief that remained made him seem ill. "Thank you," he said softly. "Felicia was one of my oldest friends. I can't imagine life without her in it."

"You must have known her well."

"She was like my sister. I met her when we were both in kindergarten." He paused a moment. "My parents were going through a phase where they wanted to prove they weren't snobs, so they sent me to public school. I met Felicia on my first day. She was the kindest person I ever knew."

"I wish I'd known her better."

"She was worth knowing well. Would you like to sit in the gazebo?" he asked. "There's more of a breeze there. I've arranged for refreshments to be brought out to us."

"That sounds nice." Kaylee followed the tall, slender man across the wide lawn. She'd been in many gazebos in her life. They were often a part of gardens, and she knew how easy it was for them to become peeling, dirty, and filled with wasp nests. The gazebo in Isaac Pine's garden, however, was pristine, holding only a glass-topped wicker table and chairs.

Isaac politely pulled out one of the chairs for Kaylee, and she sat down with Bear at her feet, setting the cookies on the table. When he took the chair across from her, Kaylee said, "Had you and Felicia dated long?"

He looked at her in stark surprise, then laughed. "Felicia and I never dated. Our relationship was more like siblings."

"But she came to the island with you," Kaylee said.

"I brought her here because she told me she was afraid of something on the mainland. She wouldn't say what she wanted to hide from, or who. I thought once she'd been here a while, she'd relax and fess up, but she never did."

"So you weren't bothered by her dating Nick?" Kaylee asked.

"Not at all. Nick seemed to be good for her. I was happy about their relationship."

A man dressed in crisp black pants and a spotless white dress shirt came out of the house carrying a large tray. His snow-white hair was so neat it almost appeared fake. The extreme neatness to everything about his appearance made the one imperfection—a wide bandage around one finger—stand out starkly.

The man quickly unloaded the tray, placing frosty glasses of lemonade in front of Kaylee and Isaac, then setting a plate piled with small sandwiches between them. The sandwiches were arranged so carefully that the presentation resembled a piece of art, especially since someone had garnished them with nasturtium petals.

The man stood up sharply and gave Isaac a blank expression. "Would you like anything else, sir?"

"This is fine. Thank you, Wallace." Isaac turned to Kaylee. "Is there anything you'd like? Wallace can bring you coffee if you'd prefer that. I like lemonade in the summer, but I know it's not everyone's favorite."

"Lemonade will be fine, thank you." Kaylee offered Wallace a smile. "The sandwiches are lovely."

The man offered her a tight nod. "I will tell the cook."

He strode away, and Isaac sighed. "My father is the one who hired the staff here. He likes a decidedly more formal relationship with them, and I cannot get Wallace to lighten up. He didn't even like Felicia, and everyone liked Felicia." Isaac sat back and took a long sip of his lemonade, then said, "You were asking how I felt about Felicia dating Nick. I thought it was great. She was clearly afraid of something, and Nick was a deputy. I thought she was probably safer with him."

"It didn't bother you that Nick wasn't exactly friendly to you?" Kaylee asked, trying to ignore that Nick himself was listening.

When Isaac raised his eyebrows in question, she ducked her head. "I saw your, um, altercation with him at O'Brien's the other day."

"I wasn't thrilled with that. But Felicia spoke highly of him, and I thought his suspicion of me probably meant he was protective. Again, I thought she'd be safe with him."

Kaylee took a sip of her lemonade to give her a moment to think through her next question. She wasn't sure how much she believed what Isaac was saying. He certainly sounded sincere, and she could see the effects of grief all over his face, but that didn't necessarily mean everything he said to her was true. Finally, she put her glass back on the table and said, "That night at O'Brien's when you wanted to talk to Felicia. What was that about?"

Isaac's mouth thinned for a moment, then he said, "I had found something on Felicia's doorstep. She was staying here on the property at an old cabin my grandmother used for an art studio many years ago. The building wasn't serving any purpose, and Felicia liked the independence of living there, especially after she started dating Nick." He laughed without humor. "I doubt Nick would have been pleased if she'd been living here at the house with me."

"No, probably not. What did you find at the cabin?"

"A bird," he said with a small shudder. "A dead bird."

"What?" Kaylee was horrified.

"I think it was some sort of seabird, but I'm no expert. I don't like birds. I'm phobic, in fact. So seeing a dead one on the doorstep, it shook me."

"Could the bird have simply flown into a window?" Kaylee asked.

"I don't think so. It wasn't near a window. It was right on the doorstep with its wings spread out like some kind of display."

"You think someone put it there intentionally?"

"I do. I tried to call Felicia to tell her about it, but her phone was off. I was very upset and probably not thinking things through like I should have. I went straight to O'Brien's because I knew that was where she and Nick were going for dinner. Obviously I didn't get to talk to her. I came right home after that and sent Wallace over to clean up the dead bird, which is what I suppose I should have done in the first place."

"You didn't think to call the police?"

Isaac picked up his lemonade again, but instead of taking a sip, he stared blankly at the glass. "I didn't think Felicia would like that. Whenever I mentioned telling the police about whatever was frightening her, she would make me swear not to. I should have done it anyway. It would have been better to have her mad at me and still alive."

"Was the bird the only odd thing to happen here?"

"The only one I can think of," he said. "The cabin is out of sight of the main house. I suppose something else could have happened and she didn't tell me."

"It sounds like Felicia was very secretive."

"That's just the thing—she wasn't. Not normally. Whatever was going on with her, it was changing her. She actively tried to keep me away from Nick. I honestly think we could have settled everything if I'd just had an open talk with him early on in their relationship."

"I heard you and Felicia went on a whale watch not long ago," Kaylee prompted.

He perked up at that. "It's such a touristy thing to do, but I really enjoyed it. I find the ocean relaxing, though that boat operator could certainly learn a bit about social interactions."

"She said you and Felicia barely paid attention to the tour at all."

He raised his eyebrows. "I wouldn't have pegged you for a gossip."

Kaylee nearly laughed. "If you think someone has to be

a gossip to hear Roz Corzo's opinions, you didn't pay much attention to her."

"I'll give you that. She *was* abrasive. The whale watch was actually Felicia's idea. She thought we could use it to talk without being overheard. We didn't talk about anything important, though. Mostly just ferry schedules. And she asked if I could watch for strangers on the island, but I don't know the people here well enough to tell who is a stranger."

"Why didn't she want to talk to you here?" Kaylee asked.

He huffed. "She didn't like Wallace. She said he was rude to her. He never treated her badly in front of me, though. The truth is that Felicia didn't trust anyone, and I'm very much afraid that may have been what got her killed."

They talked a bit longer, but Kaylee didn't get any other information. Soon, the conversation turned to the island and how beautiful it was. "I'm surprised your family opted to build so far inland," Kaylee said. "Most people like a view of the water."

Isaac gave a shrug. "My father said ocean views are simply invitations to storm damage. And Mother reminds him of that every time a pine tree on the property falls and damages something."

Kaylee took a last bite of one of the tiny sandwiches and patted her stomach. "I do appreciate the lovely lunch, but I should be getting back to work. I hope you enjoy the cookies."

Isaac rose to his feet as Kaylee stood. "Could I possibly impose upon you for one more thing? It's a favor. Kind of a big one, actually, but I suppose it's more a favor for Felicia than for me."

"Now you have me curious," Kaylee said. "What kind of favor?"

"Felicia had a pet bird. It's a parrot. It basically hates everyone other than Felicia, and Wallace told me this morning that he'll quit before he goes near that bird again." He sighed. "With my phobia, I can't even walk into the cabin. Would you consider driving by and feeding the bird? I'll pay you for your trouble."

Kaylee waved away his offer with her hand. "There's no need to pay me. My cottage isn't far from here, so I could do it until you find a new home for the bird. Where is the cabin?"

The relief that flooded the tall man's face made him suddenly appear younger. He reached into his pocket and took out a key, which he handed her. He pointed to the nearby trees. "It's right through the woods. There's a walking path, but you'll likely want to take the road so you can leave from there." He explained how to reach the cabin by a side road that branched off the long driveway Kaylee had taken up to the mansion.

"I remember seeing that side road," Kaylee said. "It's narrow and a little overgrown, right?"

Isaac nodded. "I offered to get it cleared out when Felicia moved into the cabin, but she insisted that the overgrowth made her safer. The cabin is the only thing on the road, so you'll find it without any problem."

"How likely am I to get bitten by her bird?" Kaylee asked.

"Not at all," he assured her. "He's in a cage, and you don't have to put your hands inside to fill the food dish or change the water. Wallace was bitten when he tried to clean the cage, but he said the cage looks clean enough for now anyway. I haven't seen it. Hopefully I'll have figured out what to do with the creature by the time it needs cleaning again."

"In that case, it sounds easy enough. Thank you again for lunch."

"And thank you for this favor. You don't know how much I appreciate it." He bent to pat Bear on the head and scratch his ears. "It was nice to meet you too, sir."

Bear wagged his tail as if to return the sentiment.

The narrow side road was gravel, so Kaylee took the drive slowly for the sake of her vehicle. She suspected the plentiful ruts could knock her wheels out of alignment if she tried to pick up speed. Finally, she reached the cabin.

As she would have expected, the trim little cabin was lovely, complete with flower boxes on the abundant windows. Kaylee hopped out of the car and collected Bear, snapping on his leash as she walked up to the door. She held the key in her hand but soon saw she didn't need it. The door was ajar.

"That can't be good," she whispered.

Bear stuck his nose in the crack and barked. The sharp sound was met by a resounding screech. Kaylee peeked through the door and gasped. The inside of the cabin looked as if a storm had passed through, destroying everything in its path.

11

Since she couldn't be sure the cabin was empty, and she certainly didn't plan to go inside and check, Kaylee led Bear several paces away from the building and pulled out her phone. She knew she should call the sheriff first. Anything else was wrong. But when she checked the screen, she saw that her surveillance call to Nick was still connected, so she put the phone to her ear.

"Are you still there, Nick? Someone has been in Felicia's cabin." Her voice was high and thin, and she nearly fell over the words. "The place is trashed. I need to call the sheriff."

"Wait!" Nick yelped. "Give me just a minute. I'll be right there."

"Nick, I can't do this. The sheriff's office is not going to understand my holding off on calling them."

"I'm almost there," he said. "But you're right. Go ahead and call. It'll take the sheriff's office a while to get there. I should still have a few minutes for a quick look around."

As soon as Nick ended the call, Kaylee heard another bloodcurdling screech from inside the cabin. The sound made Bear bark. "At least the bird is still alive," she said. She held the phone against her chest for a moment, taking deep breaths. She wanted to be coherent when she spoke to the sheriff's department.

Finally, she felt calm enough to make the call. She managed to get through the conversation without falling apart. As she slipped the phone back into her pocket, the brush near the cabin began to rustle, and Bear released a rapid-fire series of yaps. Kaylee scooped him up and held him to her chest as she watched the foliage, wide-eyed.

Nick stepped through, and Kaylee let out the breath she'd been holding. "Stop sneaking up on me!"

He gave her a penitent smile. "I scared you again. Sorry about that." He pointed back the way he'd come. "I was lurking in the bushes while you talked to Pine, just in case he tried something, but that meant I practically had to circle the property to get to the road here unseen."

Kaylee clutched Bear close, still waiting for the pounding of her heart to calm. At the rate this case was going, she'd have gray hair by the end. "It's all right. I should have realized that was you."

"Hold on. I'll be right back." Nick headed for the cabin. He stood in the doorway and peered around.

Kaylee slowly walked over as he surveyed the interior. "Do you see the bird? I heard it, so I know whoever broke in didn't kill it. Still, if it's hurt, I feel like I should do something."

Nick stepped to one side of the doorway and pointed. "It appears that whoever broke in didn't touch the cage."

Sure enough, Kaylee saw the large birdcage in the corner of the room. She'd missed it the first time she'd peeked in, as the mess had taken all her attention. The birdcage door was closed, and a large, blue parrot paced back and forth on a perch glaring in their direction.

"It looks okay," she said quietly. Again, the mess captured her attention. "Why would someone do this? I guess they must have been searching for something."

"Yeah, but this goes beyond a simple search." Nick tapped his foot anxiously. "Someone was angry—really angry. I'd love to poke around, but I don't want to run the risk of being caught in there when the sheriff arrives."

"Not to mention leaving evidence," Kaylee said.

He shrugged. "I've been here before, so they're already going to find my prints. Felicia was almost obsessively neat, but I'm sure there's something." Kaylee could see the pain on his face as he turned back to the mess. "She would be horrified to see the state of all her belongings." He finally backed away from the door. "I'm going to stay close, but I don't want to be found here with you. You and Bear need to stay out here, of course."

"Of course." Kaylee ran her gaze over the mess again and shuddered. Rage was clear in every shredded cushion and smashed bit of pottery. "At least the bird is okay. I imagine Felicia would be glad of that."

"She would. She loved that thing, even though it was easily the most vicious creature I've ever seen. She always had to stick him back in the cage when I was coming over or he would go after me."

Kaylee smiled a little. "And you were afraid of a bird?"

"Have you seen an angry parrot?" Nick raised an eyebrow. "The monster could nip a hunk right out of you with that beak. Don't be fooled by the pretty feathers. I'm definitely more of a dog guy." He reached out to scratch Bear's ears. "Look, I better get out of here. But I'm close. Don't worry."

"I won't. Thanks, Nick."

"Don't thank me. I'm the only reason you're facing this in the first place." He gave Bear one last pat and hopped off the tiny porch to head for the brush again.

Kaylee called out just before he reached the brush. "What's the bird's name?"

"Hero. I always told Felicia she should have called him Villain instead." Then he waved and disappeared into the brush.

Kaylee wondered if it would be all right if she sat in the rocking chair on the porch instead of waiting at her car. The chair was inviting, and she suddenly felt a bit wobbly in the knees. "I guess if it's not all right, Sheriff Maddox will just yell at me. I've survived that before." She perched on the edge of the rocker with Bear in her lap.

By the time a sheriff's department cruiser pulled up beside her Ford Escape, Kaylee had slipped back to sit more comfortably in the rocking chair and Bear had fallen asleep in her lap. He woke with a start at the sound of the car pulling in. As Sheriff Maddox emerged from the first car, a second cruiser pulled up behind it and Robyn Garcia hopped out.

"You all right, Kaylee?" the sheriff asked as he approached.

Kaylee stood, still holding Bear. "I'm fine. A little shaken at seeing that mess inside."

The sheriff's dark brows drew together. "You didn't go in, did you?"

She shook her head. "I only looked in the doorway to see if the bird was okay."

"Bird?"

"I actually came here to tend Felicia's pet parrot. Isaac is afraid of birds, so he asked me to check on him."

"That explains why he wasn't in a hurry to meet us here when we called to inform him of the situation," the sheriff said.

"The bird seems to be okay, but I would appreciate it if I could feed and water him after you're done."

"That would be fine, if you don't mind waiting while we check this out."

"I don't mind."

"Wait a second," Maddox said suspiciously. "Why did Pine ask you to check on the bird? Do you know him?"

Kaylee cast about for an innocent-sounding way to explain her presence. "I took cookies up to him to see how he was doing after Felicia's death. He asked for a favor."

"Just happened to take cookies to a man connected with a

murder investigation that I specifically told you to stay out of, huh?"

"Yes sir," Kaylee said, trying to sound more confident than she felt under the sheriff's piercing gaze. "He's seasonal, and I was concerned he might not have many local friends to help him through something like this. No one should be alone when they're grieving."

Maddox's face softened. "All right. Stay put."

She gestured to the rocker. "Can I sit here?"

"Might as well," the sheriff said. "You won't be in our way."

Kaylee settled down. She exchanged greetings with Deputy Garcia as she slipped by, carrying a case that Kaylee assumed contained equipment for gathering evidence or dusting for fingerprints. With strangers in the cabin, the bird began squawking and shrieking again.

Kaylee leaned back in the chair and closed her eyes, wishing she was back at The Flower Patch. Then she sat up sharply. Mary had to be wondering where she was since her errand was taking much longer than anticipated.

Mary picked up right away. "I was starting to worry."

"I know, I'm sorry," Kaylee said. "I decided to come out and talk to Isaac Pine. I know I shouldn't have, but I just felt like I needed to know more about him. Anyway, he asked me if I'd check on Felicia's bird. I was doing that when I found her place had been broken into. Now the sheriff is here, and I'm going to be tied up a while longer."

"Wow," Mary said. "That was a lot. You talked to Isaac Pine?"

"Yes." Kaylee was surprised that Mary latched onto that instead of the break-in. "He actually seems nice, and truly torn up over Felicia's death. But he told me he has a bird phobia, and Felicia had a pet parrot that needed feeding."

"You said there was a break-in," Mary said. "Is the bird all right? I like birds. I hate to think of someone hurting one."

"The bird seems fine, though it's really noisy. But the rest of Felicia's cabin is a mess."

"Do you think it might have been a robbery?"

"I don't know. If it was, they smashed everything they didn't steal."

"That could have been intentional. It's a good way to obscure what's missing. I remember a case years ago where there was a break-in at a jewelry store and everything was smashed for just that reason."

"That happened here?" Kaylee asked, shocked.

"In Eastsound," Mary said. "It was a long time ago."

Kaylee twisted around in the rocking chair, making Bear protest quietly, and peered back toward the door. The bird still squawked, especially whenever the sheriff or deputy walked close to the cage. *Could the mess be intended to hide something else?* She'd just have to trust the sheriff's department to sort it out. "Whatever the reason, the cabin is certainly a disaster area," she said. "And the sheriff wants to talk to me, but I don't know how long it will be before that happens."

"Well, don't worry about the shop," Mary said. "I can handle anything that might come along. You didn't have any design appointments today, did you?"

"No, not today. I do have two next week for weddings. It's about time too. We've gotten a slow start on summer weddings this year."

"I'm sure we'll be buried soon and talking wistfully of these easier days."

Kaylee glanced through the door of the cabin again. She wasn't sure this would fall under the heading of an easier day, but she was grateful that it wasn't putting her behind at work. Kaylee tried hard to avoid disappointing her clients. She thanked Mary and ended the call.

She stood, Bear in her arms, and walked over to lean on one of the porch posts and watch the activity inside the cabin. The door was fully open and gave her a view of most of the interior. She saw Deputy Garcia taking photos of the room while the sheriff poked around and wrote notes on a pad.

Maddox caught sight of Kaylee and walked over. "This is going to take some time. I don't want to hold you all day. You can go, and I'll come by the flower shop later."

"That's very kind of you," Kaylee said, "But I don't want to leave without feeding the bird and giving it water."

The sheriff turned back to the cabin with a frown. "I believe you could go ahead and do that. The bird's cage seems to be untouched, so it won't affect any evidence for you to feed it. And it might stop shrieking." As he spoke, Deputy Garcia passed by the cage and elicited an especially loud squawk.

"It doesn't seem to like anyone close to the cage," Kaylee said. "I might make it worse when I try to feed it."

"Maybe," the sheriff agreed, "but I'm open to even the possibility of the thing quieting down. Give it a try. The birdseed is on the counter in the kitchen. The intruder slashed the bag open, but I think you should still be able to get enough seed from it."

"Do you think the intruder expected to find something hidden in a bag of birdseed?" Kaylee asked.

"I can't tell how much of this is a search and how much is simply a temper tantrum." Sheriff Maddox sighed. "Let me get you some booties for your shoes and you can come in." He nodded toward Bear. "But I'm afraid he has to stay outside."

"No problem," Kaylee said. "He can wait here on the porch where it's cool. I'll just tie his leash to the rail."

"That will be fine." He walked back inside while Kaylee secured Bear to the railing.

When she was done, she patted him on the head. "I'll only

be a minute. I promise." Bear licked her hand and Kaylee stood, turning toward the door.

Deputy Garcia waited in the doorway. "Give that squawking monster plenty to eat," she said as she handed Kaylee the booties, a touch of humor in her voice. "The longer he has a mouthful of food, the longer our ears will get a break."

Kaylee walked over to the cage, earning a fresh round of enraged squawks. Rather than pulling out the food dish right away, she spoke quietly to the bird. "I know, Hero. This is all very upsetting." To her surprise, the bird stopped squawking and peered at her with his black, beady eyes. "I miss Felicia too. Poor fellow. You were her hero. That's a nice name." She continued cooing at the bird while it listened attentively.

"I don't know about the bird, but you are officially *our* hero," Robyn said.

Hero screeched at the deputy.

Kaylee got the parrot's attention again with some more sweet talk. He was a large bird with brilliant blue feathers other than a yellow ring around each eye and a yellow stripe at the side of his black beak. The beak looked strong and sharp, and with the bird's temperament, Kaylee couldn't blame Wallace for not wanting to clean the cage.

She examined the rest of the enclosure as she continued crooning at the bird. The cage was relatively clean except for a smear of something on the bars of the door. She leaned closer, then gasped. "Sheriff?" she said quietly. "There's blood on the cage door."

"Blood?" Deputy Garcia repeated.

The sheriff and deputy both walked over. The bird fluffed up and opened his dark beak for a single squawk, then fell silent again.

"Sheriff," Robyn said, pointing, "there's blood on the floor here too."

"Is the bird bleeding?" the sheriff asked.

Kaylee bent lower and risked the bird's wrath by putting her face close to the cage. "I don't see any blood, and it would show on those feathers. I think this blood belongs to someone who put his hand in the cage." Then she groaned. "I know whose it might be."

"Who?" the sheriff demanded sharply.

Hero squawked loudly at the sheriff's tone, making Kaylee jump.

"Isaac Pine said his butler came over to clean the parrot's cage," she explained. "Since he wouldn't have needed to do that if Felicia was alive, he must have been here just before whoever trashed the place. Mr. Pine said he refuses to have anything to do with the bird now, so he probably got bitten. I saw a bandage on his hand."

"Would he have simply left the blood on the floor?" the sheriff asked.

Kaylee considered that. She remembered the almost military precision of the man and his immaculate clothes. He didn't seem like someone who could walk away from a mess. "Good point. Although he may have left in a hurry to tend to his wound. Either that, or the bird has potentially made two people bleed in a short time."

"Or Mr. Pine's servant took out his anger on the cabin." Maddox glanced around. "And he would have to have a lot of anger. Did you get the man's name?"

"Wallace," Kaylee said. "I don't know if that's a first or last name."

"I'll find out," Deputy Garcia said.

"Let's collect samples of this blood," the sheriff said. "If there's none on the food dish, you can go ahead with feeding it." He frowned at the cage. "The nasty creature certainly seems to like you."

"Maybe it's because you look so much like Felicia," Robyn

suggested as she pulled some swabs out of her evidence kit for the blood.

Kaylee didn't comment. She still didn't see the resemblance as being particularly close. As soon as she got the go ahead, she slid the little door for the food dish open. The bird watched her sharply, but he made no move to attack. For whatever reason, the parrot liked her. Or at least hated her less than everyone else.

She padded to the kitchen, the booties on her feet swishing against the floor. The bag of birdseed lay on the counter, spilling its contents into the sink. Kaylee carefully filled the dish and took it back to the cage. The bird immediately rushed over and began eating as soon as the dish was in place.

"Oh, you poor thing," Kaylee cooed. "You were hungry, weren't you? No wonder you were so cranky." She wondered if Wallace had fed the bird or if parrots simply ate a lot. She'd have to come out daily to make sure it got enough to eat. She rinsed out the water dish at the sink and filled it. Once she was done with the bird, she said, "I'll be going now. Unless you need anything else?"

"I think we're good," the sheriff said. "I'll be speaking to Isaac Pine before I come to the shop, so it may be late afternoon."

"I'll be there."

Kaylee started for the door, then saw Bear. It appeared that he'd been pulling on the leash the whole time she'd been inside, and Kaylee could see he'd worked it mostly loose from the railing. He'd spotted her coming toward the door and strained against the leash. "No, Bear," she called. "Stay there."

The leash knot slipped loose and Bear raced for the door. To Kaylee's relief, he didn't come inside, but merely stopped at the doorframe and sniffed eagerly. She raced to intercept him.

As she bent to pick up the sniffing dachshund, she caught sight of something she hadn't been able to see from outside. Scooping up Bear, she turned back toward Deputy Garcia. "There's some plant matter caught in the crack in the floor here at the entryway. It reminds me of something else I've seen recently."

The deputy walked over to collect the sample, and the sheriff peered at it. "There's a lot of overgrowth around this cabin," he said. "I imagine Felicia tracked in something every time she came and went."

"True, but I saw just this kind of mix recently. I would have to see it under a microscope to tell you the exact plant makeup, but it appears to be very similar to a bit of soil and plant matter I saw in the restroom sink at Death by Chocolate."

The sheriff's expression stayed skeptical. "We're on an island with a lot of plants. What are the odds of a connection between the bakery and this cabin?"

"Point taken," Kaylee admitted. "It sounds silly, but the circumstances at the bakery have stayed with me because they were so peculiar." Despite the skepticism on the sheriff's face, she told him about William Tomlinson's collapse in the men's room and the strange placement of dirt and plants on the edge of the sink under the window.

"Maybe he crawled out the window to sneak a cigarette," Deputy Garcia suggested. The sheriff and Kaylee both turned to gape at her, and the deputy shrugged. "When I was in high school, the girls' restroom had a sink right under the window. You weren't allowed to smoke in the school, and some of the wilder girls would stand on the sink so they could stick their heads out the window and smoke." She looked from the sheriff to Kaylee. "Not me, of course."

"Of course," the sheriff said. "I still don't see any reason to consider a volunteer with a teen program as a suspect in this cabin break-in. But we've got the evidence, and I appreciate you spotting it. You can go on back to work, Kaylee."

Kaylee felt as thought she'd essentially gotten a patronizing pat on the head. The sheriff couldn't have made it clearer that he wasn't taking her seriously.

Kaylee mulled over Robyn's story as she headed out of the cabin. Had William stood on the sink to reach the window? And if so, why? With a sigh, she headed out of the cabin, realizing that she didn't have a single answer to the questions popping up all around her.

12

When Kaylee got back to the shop, Mary's relief was obvious. "Has it been a tough afternoon?" Kaylee asked. "Did Pepper leave?"

"She had to join the Learners on Location group, though she seemed reluctant to leave. She's certainly taken a shine to flower arranging," Mary said, a note of pride in her voice. "And the afternoon was busy. I sold all but one of the little arrangements that Pepper made. They weren't expensive, of course, but I know she'll be happy." She wagged a finger at Kaylee. "Don't try to distract me with shoptalk. I can't believe you went to see Isaac Pine. What did you think of him? And tell me about the cabin."

Kaylee laughed. "I'll be happy to. Isaac Pine seems very nice and honestly distraught about Felicia, but he has a man working for him who might warrant a second thought." She explained how Isaac had sent Wallace to Felicia's cabin. "Surely Wallace wasn't expected to clean a birdcage when Felicia was alive, so that means he had to have just been out there. And maybe he was the one looking for something."

"So the cabin was searched?" Mary asked.

"Searched and destroyed," Kaylee said. "The only thing in the place that was untouched was the parrot's cage, though there was a sign someone had tried. There was blood on the cage and in front of it, but the bird showed no sign of a wound. If the parrot can give a bite that nasty, I am not surprised the intruder left him alone."

"Sounds like the intruder wasn't wearing gloves if the parrot was able to draw blood," Mary said. "Maybe the sheriff will find prints."

"That would be good, although the blood may have belonged to Isaac's butler. He got bit earlier." Kaylee sighed. "This is all so sad. I actually felt bad for the bird. He calmed down a little when I talked to him. I've heard parrots are very smart. He's probably waiting for Felicia to come home." She smiled down at Bear who was chewing on a treat Mary had slipped him. "I can't imagine how Bear would react if something happened to me. At least I have people who would help me take care of him."

"You know it."

Kaylee shook off her burst of melancholy. "I can finish up for the day. I certainly made you stay on your own long enough."

"I could use a run to the grocery store before I get home. Herb has been hinting about steaks on the grill." Mary grabbed her purse and then paused. "I don't want to overstep, but it might be better if you stay clear of the investigation." Kaylee opened her mouth, but Mary held up a hand to stop her protest. "I know you feel bad for Nick and you liked Felicia, but I worry about you getting involved. And I know the sheriff couldn't have been happy to find you at the cabin."

"Surprisingly, he didn't scold me," Kaylee said. "But he did say he'd come by here to take my statement. I'll likely get my scolding then."

"Probably. I just hope you pay attention." Then Mary smiled at her to soften the reproach, handed Bear another treat, and left for the day.

Kaylee laughed at Bear's hopeful face. "No more treats. You're going to turn into an overstuffed sausage."

Bear seemed to understand. He settled down behind the counter while Kaylee started on some paperwork.

The next hour was unusually quiet, until a short, stocky man walked in, his lips pressed tightly together.

"May I help you?" Kaylee asked.

"Yeah, I need an arrangement. Something small and not too expensive."

Kaylee led him to the cooler and brought out the last of the little arrangements Pepper had done. It was a cute little design made entirely of leftover blooms cut for the Learners on Location program. The flowers had all had short stems which made them challenging to use, but Pepper had tucked them into a seashell that Kaylee had found on the shore of one of the small islands around Orcas.

The man barely glanced at the bouquet. "That'll be fine."

"Great," Kaylee said, then carried the small arrangement to the counter to ring it up.

The man pulled out his wallet and said, "I came to Orcas Island expecting a quiet week away from the stress of the city, and I find out there's been a murder. Is no place safe?"

"Orcas Island—and Turtle Cove especially—is a warm, safe place. Unfortunately, no place is magic."

The man harrumphed as he handed over cash for the arrangement. "I heard the victim was a tourist. You don't think someone is after visitors to the island?"

"I'm sure that's not the case," Kaylee replied with as much conviction as she could muster.

He didn't exactly perk up, but he didn't grumble anymore either. He took his flowers and left.

Kaylee was watching after him when she spotted a familiar figure striding down the sidewalk outside the flower shop. She hurried out onto the porch. "Roz!" she called. "Can you spare a minute?"

Roz Corzo used a forearm to shield her eyes from the sun as she squinted toward Kaylee. "I suppose. I could use a few minutes off my feet."

With no customers left in the shop, Kaylee gestured to the rocking chairs on the porch. Roz stomped up the steps in her heavy fishing boots and practically flopped into the closest seat.

Kaylee winced, glad that the furniture handled the aggressive landing without a groan. She took the chair beside Roz's. "I wanted to ask you something about a whale watch you took. The one with Isaac Pine and Felicia Lewis."

Roz narrowed her eyes. "What about it? I heard about that girl dying." She shook her head. "Must have been rough running up on her in a coffin like that."

"It *was* distressing," Kaylee admitted. "You had told me that Isaac and Felicia were very absorbed in one another during the whale watch. Did they actually do anything romantic, like hugging or kissing?"

Roz wrinkled her nose. "No, thankfully. I get enough couples like that. Sometimes I take out a whole group, and we'll have one couple that thinks that stuff is something everyone wants to see and hear."

"But they were whispering?" Kaylee asked.

Roz shrugged. "No, not really. Talking quiet enough that I couldn't hear them, but you don't have to whisper to do that. Boats are noisy. They were having an intense conversation, but not like she was mad at him or anything." Her expression turned shrewd. "Why do you ask? You think he might have killed her?"

"I don't know who killed her. But he seems like a nice man."

Roz's spark of interest waned. "Yeah, he was really polite. I'll give him that. And he paid cash. I like cash." Then she barked out a laugh. "Maybe they were planning a bank robbery. That would be a good way to put a little more cash in their pockets."

"I don't really think they were the bank robber types."

Roz lifted broad shoulders in a shrug. "Who knows? Well, I gotta go. No rest for the weary business owner."

Kaylee watched Roz stomp away, wondering about the secrets Felicia had kept and which one of them got her killed.

She didn't have long to think about it, however, as Sheriff Maddox showed up to take her statement. With a sigh, Kaylee went over her visit to the cabin again, feeling the rush of guilt at leaving out so much of the truth about Nick. She hoped the sheriff found the killer soon. The burden of secrets was weighing heavy on her.

Kaylee found she felt much better by Thursday morning, despite the upsetting moments of the day before. For one thing, Reese was coming home. Though she and Reese were just friends—despite what the Petal Pushers thought—Kaylee had missed the handyman's company. She had also missed his steadying influence on Nick. The two men were good friends, and Kaylee hoped Nick might listen to Reese when it came to investigating Felicia's death.

When she got to The Flower Patch, she let Bear in and greeted Mary. "I thought I'd start our day right and run next door for coffee and treats."

"Sounds like a delicious idea," Mary agreed. "I'll watch Bear."

As soon as Kaylee got to Death by Chocolate, she noticed something very familiar. The small seashell arrangement she'd sold the afternoon before sat beside the register next to Oliver's pot. "I recognize that bouquet," she said to Jessica. "Pepper made it."

Jessica raised both eyebrows. "Really? That makes it even more special. One of the summer visitors gave it to me yesterday afternoon. He said he wanted to show me how much he appreciated the coffee and pastries he'd gotten here during his stay. Isn't that darling?"

Kaylee agreed that it was very sweet. It was also surprising. The man hadn't seemed like someone given to spontaneous displays of appreciation. *You just never really know about people, I guess.*

Jessica asked Kaylee which pastries she wanted, pulling her out of her distracted thoughts. She considered all the delicious-looking offerings in the case, then picked out a few filled croissants.

As Jessica loaded the pastries into a box, she said, "That Pepper is such a bright girl. She did wonderfully during the baking demonstration yesterday afternoon."

"Oh that's right," Kaylee said. "I'm sorry I missed it. I meant to pop over and watch a little, but I got caught up elsewhere. I do find the enthusiasm those teens have is infectious."

"It is. And it reinvigorated my love for baking. They had so many questions and suggestions." Jessica laughed. "They certainly aren't shy about giving their opinions."

"As long as they aren't rude, good for them."

"Absolutely," Jessica agreed. Then her smile grew a little sly. "So, I heard about what caught you up elsewhere." She leaned forward and dropped her voice to a whisper. "Who do you think broke into Felicia's cabin?"

"Where did you possibly hear about that?" Kaylee asked.

"Mary. You had her worried half to death." Jessica pointed at the geranium. "And Oliver was worried as well. He actually dropped a leaf."

Kaylee was tempted to ask if that might have been caused by the little floral arrangement crowded up beside the geranium, but she knew better than to question Jessica's belief in Oliver's psychic abilities. "I was fine. I was only doing a favor by feeding Felicia's pet parrot. Whoever made a mess of Felicia's cabin was long gone by the time I got there."

"And you have no guesses about who it was?" Jessica asked.

"I think it might have been Isaac Pine. He's always been very nice, but you never know about people."

Kaylee was startled to hear Jessica voice a thought she'd had only minutes before. She'd liked Isaac when she met him, but could she have misjudged him? Was Isaac's story of being a good friend to Felicia just that—a story? Had Kaylee been chatting with a killer?

13

Kaylee's preoccupation with the week's odd events kept her quiet as she worked on arrangements for an anniversary party. The couple made regular visits to the island, and Kaylee had spent hours on the phone and in video chats as the wife chose designs and then second-guessed herself several times. She'd finally promised not to change her mind anymore, though Kaylee thought the promise sounded strained. She certainly hoped the arrangement she was making would end up at the party on Friday.

"I guess I'll know tomorrow when they come in on the ferry," she said softly to herself.

"Did you say something?" Mary asked.

Kaylee felt her cheeks flush. She hadn't heard Mary walk over from the front counter.

"I was talking to myself," she admitted. "Mrs. Bryson has changed her mind about these arrangements so many times."

"This arrangement is gorgeous," Mary assured her. "I'm sure she'll be delighted."

Kaylee turned the finished bouquet in a slow circle, checking for any blooms out of place. "I hope so."

"Are you feeling all right? You seem down. I know yesterday was stressful."

"Maybe a little. This summer has felt strange somehow. The seasonal visitors are always a mixed blessing, but I guess it all feels a little extra ominous lately."

"Well, I know exactly what will cheer you up," Mary said. She pointed at the clock on the wall. "If you hurry, you can catch the ferry and greet Reese. I'm sure a nice chat with him will help you clear your head."

Kaylee peered at Mary with her hands on her hips, examining her friend's face for signs of matchmaking. "I *would* like to talk with him about Nick."

"I think that's wise," Mary said decisively. "Reese will want to know, and he may be better at helping Nick cope with Felicia's death than we would be. Sometimes a male friend simply understands better."

The thought of walking down to the ferry sounded wonderful, but Kaylee gestured back at the arrangement. "I still have one more of these to put together."

"And no one will be picking them up until tomorrow. You'll have plenty of time after you meet Reese and have a nice long chat. I expect you'll find it much easier to work once you've cleared out a few cobwebs." Mary picked up the arrangement from the table. "I'll take this to the cooler."

"You may be right," Kaylee said. "And I know Bear would like to see Reese." At the sound of his name, Bear jumped to his feet and ran in circles around Kaylee and Mary. They chuckled at his antics.

"I believe Bear is voting for the walk to the ferry," Mary said. "Though I'm not sure how I'll get to the cooler with Bear pretending we're a racetrack."

Kaylee crouched down to grab Bear on his next pass in front of her. "Come on, silly boy. Let's go meet Reese." Kaylee wondered how she could ever feel down with Bear around. She carried him out to the front counter, retrieved his leash, and snapped it on his collar.

As she and Bear stepped out on the porch, Kaylee blinked at the bright sunshine. She started down the steps and reached the sidewalk at the same moment as a familiar Flower Patch customer—the sweet husband who came each day to buy blooms for his wife.

"Running a little late today." He looked up toward the shop anxiously. "Please don't tell me you've closed for lunch or something."

"No, not at all," Kaylee said with a smile. She saw Bear sniff the man's white sneakers enthusiastically and tugged the leash gently. She knew that some people weren't quite thrilled with Bear's avid attention to scent. "Mary is inside."

"Great." The man cast a vague smile down at Bear. "See you both later." He took a step back from the dachshund, who still seemed interested in the man's shoes, then nodded and dashed up the steps.

Kaylee bent to scold Bear mildly. "A little less sniffing next time, okay?"

Bear wagged his tail cheerfully, but Kaylee doubted it was agreement. She gently straightened his blue bow tie and set off for the ferry dock. She glanced into shop windows as she passed. Everyone always went all out during the summer to catch visitors' attention, and the shop windows displayed the quirky creativity that their island community offered. When she paused to examine the display of books in Between the Lines, she caught sight of DeeDee at the window and waved.

Farther down the street, Kaylee spotted a plush lobster clutching kitchen tools in its large claws while a furry, blue crab peeked out of a pot. She chuckled at the window display, thinking the shop owners were certainly creative and whimsical. In another window, mannequins wore jaunty seaside outfits while a life-size, hand-carved wooden loon looked them over skeptically from one corner. Kaylee giggled at the sight, making Bear glance up at her quizzically. "I'm not sure they meant to imply their clothing choices were loony," Kaylee told him.

He wagged his tail as if he enjoyed her joke.

To her surprise, the window shopping seemed to be lifting some of the pall that had fallen over her mood. *Maybe I just needed a little exercise after all.*

As she neared the ferry dock, the traffic on the sidewalk slowed and Kaylee stood on tiptoe, wondering what was causing the crowd to collect. She soon spotted the problem. A large group was gathered close to the ferry landing, all snapping photos. At first Kaylee wondered if they were taking photos of the ferry coming in, but then a thin, high-pitched call rang out that Kaylee recognized immediately. It came from one of the bald eagles that lived on the island. *One of them must be fishing again,* Kaylee thought, remembering Felicia's delight at the same event. Was that really only a few days ago?

Since Kaylee suspected the hard-core bird-watchers who frequented the island were unlikely to budge as long as the eagle was providing a photo op, she scanned the area for an alternate route around the knot of people. She decided to use the ferry parking lot as a detour. She scooped up Bear so she'd be able to maneuver better, then slipped between and around people until she could dart off into the parking lot.

She wove her way between cars, still holding Bear to keep him safe in what was about to become a busy lot. Then she spotted something that made her stop. Parked between a low-slung, flashy convertible and a tiny, white hybrid was a blue sedan. The sight sent a chill down her back. Was it the car that had nearly run her over?

She slowly walked closer, peering inside to be sure no one sat in the driver's seat. The car was empty. As her heart beat faster, she hugged Bear closer and walked around the car. She realized she might be acting silly. Blue sedans weren't exactly rare. How could she be sure this was even the same vehicle? The car had flashed by so fast that she'd barely registered any details about it. Maybe her imagination was playing tricks on her.

Kaylee peered though the driver's side window, not sure what she expected to see. *It's not like whoever drives this car would have a checklist of people he intends to run over.* The sedan was very clean inside, but there were no unique features. She circled around to the back, noting the license number, then pulled her phone out of her purse.

She paused, gripping the phone. *I'm being silly.* The sheriff certainly wouldn't send someone to investigate a random sedan. Then she thought of someone who might be willing to consider her discovery.

Nick answered her call immediately. "Kaylee, I've been meaning to talk to you. Do you have any more to tell me about Felicia's cabin? Did the sheriff find anything unusual?"

Kaylee was momentarily confused, then realized that it was natural for Nick to assume her call was about the cabin. "The whole place was a mess, other than the birdcage. I think the cage was only left untouched because Hero bites."

"He didn't bite you, did he?"

"I think he actually kind of liked me," Kaylee said. "But I saw blood on the cage and on the floor near it. Someone had put a hand too close and gotten a nasty bite. I saw a bandage on the hand of a man named Wallace who works for the Pine family, but I can't really imagine him leaving blood on the floor of a cottage belonging to the family."

"Maybe he didn't notice. He might have found the pain a little distracting."

"Maybe. I didn't actually call you about the cabin, though. I might have found the car that ran me off the road, and since it might also be the car that nearly hit Felicia, I thought you'd want to know."

"Of course," Nick answered, his voice eager. "Where is it?"

"In the parking lot at the ferry. I've checked it over, and I don't see anything unusual."

"What's the license number?" he asked.

Kaylee rattled it off.

"Good. I think I can get someone to run that for me, even with my present non-status. I don't suppose you could keep an eye on the car and see who gets in it?"

"I was actually planning to meet the ferry," she said. "Reese is coming back today."

"That's right. Well, he's certainly coming back to a mess. Tell him that I'll call him this evening, will you? And I'm on my way over now, so I can watch the car."

"Good. I should go. I don't want to miss the ferry."

They ended the call and Kaylee continued to weave her way around the cars. At the edge of the parking lot, a small building served as a security station.

Near the station, she spotted a short, stocky man who seemed vaguely familiar. He was talking agitatedly to someone who was just out of sight behind the small building. She realized it was the customer who'd bought Pepper's flower arrangement and then given it to Jessica. The memory brought a small smile to Kaylee's lips. She would have stopped to tell him what a nice gesture that had been, but the man didn't appear to be in the mood for a compliment, judging by the furious expression on his face.

The person hidden by the security hut reached out and poked the man in the chest. Kaylee was getting close enough to hear the man shouting at the mystery person not to touch him.

The anger in the man's tone must have reached Bear because he growled as Kaylee held him against her chest. "Hush," she said softly. "It's all right. He's not talking to us."

Kaylee heard the voice of the hidden person and was surprised to realize it was a woman. In near shrieks, she insisted that the man didn't know who he was dealing with, but that he would. Kaylee blinked. Something about the voice was familiar. She'd definitely heard it before. She picked up her pace, hoping to reach the edge of the parking lot where the security building would no longer block her view of the speaker.

Suddenly, the man turned away from the hut and stormed toward Kaylee. She froze. His gaze flashed toward her for an instant, but if he recognized her, he gave no sign of it. She took a deep breath, scolding herself inwardly for being so jumpy, and continued on.

When she reached the edge of the parking lot, she peered at the security hut, but the woman was long gone. Who had it been? Whoever it was, she was livid. Kaylee thought of the one woman she knew who was angry virtually all the time, and especially angry toward island visitors—Roz Corzo. Kaylee mentally replayed the angry shouting, comparing it to Roz's voice. She didn't think it matched, though she wasn't sure. Thankfully Roz had never actually shouted at her.

With a sigh, Kaylee realized that whoever it was, it really wasn't any of her business. She barely knew the man, and it was time she stopped letting everything that seemed slightly out of the ordinary upset her. "Let's go see Reese," she said to Bear, then picked up her pace to the ferry landing.

She wove her way through the crowd of people waiting on the ferry and spotted Jenna Olsen striding in the opposite direction. Kaylee was suddenly struck with recognition. The voice she'd heard had been Jenna's. But what could have made Jenna shout at that man? Did the young woman have a dark side Kaylee hadn't seen?

14

Hugging Bear against her, Kaylee glanced toward the dock. The ferry still wasn't in sight, so she had a few minutes. She closed the distance between them and called out, "Jenna!"

The Learners on Location leader turned and her face lit up with her usual glowing smile. For a moment, Kaylee questioned whether this could possibly be the same person who'd just finished yelling at someone, but she pressed on. "I thought that was you I saw near the security hut. Who was that man? Is he part of the Learners on Location program?"

Jenna wrinkled her nose. "Hardly. He's some tourist, I think." She stopped and giggled. "Though I guess I'm some tourist too, aren't I?" She leaned closer to Kaylee and dropped her voice to a conspiratorial whisper. "That guy actually hit on me. Can you believe it? Do I seem like a woman who could be picked up in a parking lot? I told him exactly what I thought of that kind of behavior." She thrust her chin out. "He clearly didn't realize the sort of woman he was talking to. I'm a teacher, for goodness sake."

"Sounds like you told him."

"You know it." Then she switched her attention to Bear and cooed, "Too bad all men aren't as charming as this little guy. Hi, Bear." She scratched Bear under the chin, making him close his eyes in bliss.

"Where are the kids?" Kaylee asked, her gaze sweeping the bustling dock. "I don't see the group van."

"They're with William this morning," Jenna said. "Deputy Nick came out and gave a lesson in tracking the other day, so they all wanted to wander around in the woods for a while. I thought it was about time William pulled his weight with a physical activity, so he's leading the hike. I left him the group van and brought the rental car we had to get in order to fit everyone." Jenna laughed. "Once we had all our stuff piled up by the van, we realized we needed another set of wheels."

"Amazing how much gear it takes to live simply," Kaylee said with a smile. "I'm glad you could take some time for yourself."

"It's so beautiful here. Would you believe I saw an eagle this morning?"

"That eagle created quite a traffic jam here on the dock. I wonder if they know how popular they are. Have the kids seen the eagles?"

"I'm not sure. Is there some spot that's particularly good for seeing them? We really should make sure they catch sight of the eagles while we're here." Then before Kaylee could answer her question, Jenna continued. "By the way, thank you so much for the extra time you're giving Pepper. She was positively glowing when she rejoined the group yesterday."

"Pepper is a joy to be around, and her arrangements were quite a hit. In fact, the man you were talking to bought one of them."

"Then I guess he's not all bad, but I'm still glad I yelled at him."

Kaylee glanced toward the dock and finally saw the ferry. "I'm glad I ran into you, but I need to go. I'm meeting my friend, Reese, who's coming in on the ferry. He's actually going to do a Learners on Location presentation on creating furniture from reclaimed materials."

"That should be interesting. Tell him I'm very eager to see it." Jenna bounced on her toes. "Maybe I should wait with you and meet him."

Kaylee would have preferred to talk to Reese alone, but she didn't want to be rude. "That'd be fine. Are you sure you can stay away from the kids so long? The ferry hasn't docked yet. It might be a while."

Jenna checked her watch. "You're right. I should get going." She flashed her bright smile. "I'll meet him at the presentation anyway. I really should go rescue William before he and the kids all get horribly lost." She gave Bear a last pat on the head. "See you both later."

Kaylee watched the young woman bounce away and wondered how she could possibly have been suspicious of Jenna. *I'm getting way too paranoid.*

When she reached the waiting area for the ferry, the boat was nearly to the dock, and Kaylee felt a little flutter of excited anticipation. She'd missed Reese and his levelheaded view of life, especially the last few days.

Around her, the air was full of cheerful chatter from others meeting the ferry and a few who planned to leave the island on it. Kaylee heard one woman moan about how much she was going to miss Orcas Island. *I would too.* When she'd first taken over the flower shop from her grandmother and moved into Wildflower Cottage, Kaylee had expected to miss the city. Now she knew that if she were to return to the mainland, it would be Orcas Island that pulled at her heart.

Finally, the ferry docked and Kaylee bounced up on her toes to see over the group and watch for Reese. When she spotted him, she called out his name.

Reese turned toward her voice, but it was clear from his searching expression that he was having trouble picking her out of the crowd. "Kaylee?" he called.

"Over here!" Kaylee jumped up and down, waving to attract his attention.

Reese must have seen her then as his face cleared and he navigated toward her. He carried a worn duffel bag over one shoulder and wore what Kaylee thought of as his summer uniform—jeans and a T-shirt. On breezy days, he often added a flannel shirt.

"Phew, look at this crowd," Reese said when he reached her. "I think I could have timed my return better."

"It's good to have you back," Kaylee responded. She clung to Bear, who wriggled in joy at the sight of his friend.

Reese steered Kaylee toward an opening in the sea of people. "Let's get out of this crowd so I can breathe. That way I can give Bear the greeting I know he's hoping for."

Once they were clear of the masses, Reese hefted his bag higher on his shoulder and rubbed Bear's ears with his free hand. "It's nice to be home."

"I'm sure." Kaylee pressed her lips together as she thought of what to say next. "I'd like to catch you up on things. Do you have a minute for a cup of coffee?"

"Actually I haven't had lunch," he said. "Let's walk over to Pete's Grill if you haven't eaten yet. My treat."

Kaylee realized that she hadn't had anything since breakfast. "That sounds great." Then she sagged slightly. "But I don't think they'll let Bear in."

"I'll go in and place an order to go," he said. "We can eat at one of the picnic tables down the way."

She grinned. "Thanks. That will be nice."

Since they were finally out of the crowd, Kaylee put Bear down so he could prance along just ahead of them as they walked to the restaurant. Along the way, Kaylee told Reese the bare bones about Felicia and Nick.

"I saw something in the news about the girl's murder, but I didn't realize she was Nick's girlfriend," Reese said. "Her death must have hit him hard."

"It has. And harder still because he isn't supposed to help

with the investigation."

Reese gave her a sideways glance. "Knowing Nick, I can't imagine him staying completely out of it."

Kaylee sighed. "He hasn't." She looked down at her feet, feeling guilty. "And I've helped." She told him about Nick's requests and her compliance with them.

"I wouldn't expect anything else from you. You've got a good heart, but it can get you into sticky situations."

"I don't know how I could stay out of it," she said. "I barely knew Felicia, but I liked her. I take it you never met her?"

"No, but Nick told me about her before I left. It sounded like she was a little mysterious, and Nick can't resist that."

They reached Pete's Grill, and Kaylee waited outside on a bench with Bear as Reese went in to pick up lunch. A light breeze stirred her hair, and she admired the flowers in a low planter nearby. Though the plants were crowded a bit more than was completely healthy for them, Kaylee could see they were well-watered. If she breathed deeply, she could catch a hint of their faint sweet scent along with the sea air.

Reese came out of the restaurant with a bag and gestured toward the nearest picnic table. Kaylee and Bear followed him over. Once they were seated and served, Reese said, "Do you think the sheriff really suspects Nick?" He took a bite of his roast beef sandwich.

Kaylee pushed around the greens in her salad and shook her head. "No. But he has to be careful to be impartial. And he can't let Nick near any evidence. It could ruin a case in court."

"But you're still helping Nick?"

"I know he'll poke around even if I don't. I guess I'm hoping to keep him out of trouble."

Reese chuckled. "Because you have such a good track record of keeping out of trouble." He pinched a small bit of roast beef from his sandwich and tossed it to Bear, who caught it in the air.

Kaylee chose to ignore the teasing. "You're as bad as Mary for spoiling Bear."

"But I'm not around him as much. And I have to do something to maintain my status as Bear's favorite."

"I don't think you have to worry," Kaylee said, then her smile slipped away. "You know, the real problem is that I'm not sure the sheriff has any other suspects. I think he was considering Isaac Pine, but I met the man and I like him."

"Yeah, I know Isaac. He's a nice guy, but not very social. Honestly, I think he's shy. His family can be a little overbearing, especially for a quiet person like Isaac. I didn't know about Felicia though. Isaac said he and Felicia were old friends?"

"From the mainland," she said. "Apparently since they were kids."

Reese took a sip from his bottle of lemonade before speaking again. "Maybe he knew her from before the adoption."

Kaylee stared at him. "Adoption?"

"Yeah, the Pines adopted him when they found out they couldn't have a kid of their own. Isaac said they chose an older kid so they wouldn't have the bother of diapers and such. Apparently the first years of his life were pretty rough." He hitched a shoulder. "Though being adopted into a family that demands a lot of you can be tough too, in its own way."

Kaylee thought about that for a moment. "He said he knew Felicia from public school. He told me the Pines sent him to public school to show they were just like regular folks, but if I remember right, he hesitated before telling me that."

"You think he was lying?"

"I think he might have been covering up his early years before the Pines adopted him." Kaylee shrugged. "He didn't know me, so I suppose I can understand him not wanting to share his whole life history."

"Honestly, Kaylee, I think Isaac is just a man in need of a little peace," Reese said. "I imagine that's why he comes to Orcas Island."

"He certainly hasn't found much peace here recently."

"No he hasn't." Reese laid his sandwich down in the thick paper wrapper and stretched. "I can tell you that I'm glad to be back on the island. The air is just different here. So, tell me what the Learners on Location program has been like. You've already done your presentation, right?"

Thinking about the tangle of Felicia's death and Nick's efforts to investigate made her anxious, so Kaylee was glad for the change of topic. "The Learners on Location are great. And full of amazing ideas."

"I'm glad to hear it. I'll need to go home before I head out to the campground. I've been collecting wooden pallets and driftwood for weeks, as well as some salvage material that I picked up over at the Tortoiseshell Hotel. They're doing a huge remodel, and I was able to get the original spindles from an old back staircase they're modernizing. I guess the original banister didn't fit the fire code."

"Sounds like you've put a lot of time into this."

"That's the thing about building furniture from recycled materials," Reese said with a laugh. "You have to have recycled materials. I've also got a huge jar of sea glass for the kids to use to embellish their projects."

"What are you going to have them make?" she asked. "They'll have to take it back on the ferry, you know."

"Yeah, another complication," he said, then he grinned. "I have a couple ideas. Maybe you should come to the presentation and see for yourself."

"I'd love to, but I don't know if I can. I've been taking advantage of Mary's good heart enough lately." With a sigh, she popped the lid back on her salad. "In fact, I should get to the shop. It's really good to have you back."

"It's really good to be back." Reese's expression darkened for a moment. "You be careful helping Nick. I wouldn't want to see you hurt."

Kaylee's cheeks warmed at the sincerity in his voice, and she mumbled something in reply before gathering her things. "Good luck with the presentation."

"Hope to see you there," he said.

When Kaylee got back to The Flower Patch, Mary didn't seem the least annoyed by the time Kaylee had spent away. "Since you're back, though," Mary said, "I might slip into the kitchen and eat my lunch. I started a really good murder mystery set in Maine last night and couldn't quite finish it. I'm fairly sure I can get through the last chapter while eating my tuna sandwich."

"Take your time," Kaylee said. "Don't come back until you know who done it."

As soon as Mary disappeared into the kitchen, a handful of customers entered the shop. Kaylee recognized two of the women as part of the group that had come off the same ferry as Reese. "May I help you?" she asked.

"We're just browsing," one woman said as she pushed sunglasses up onto the top of her head.

"There are so many adorable shops here," another added, and Kaylee noticed she already carried several bags from stores between the ferry port and The Flower Patch.

"There are," Kaylee said. "Imagine the temptation I face on a daily basis."

The women chuckled at Kaylee's remark and continued browsing. In the end, one bought some of DeeDee's handmade goat milk soap that Kaylee proudly sold, and the other purchased a small silk arrangement in a mug.

The woman with the sunglasses on top of her head mildly scolded, "I don't know how you're going to keep that from getting crumpled before we get home, Tru."

Tru shrugged. "It'll be fine. And I couldn't leave it behind. It wanted me. I could tell."

Kaylee smiled at that as she finished ringing up the order. "You should meet my friend Jess. She is certain her geranium has feelings too."

"They feel more than we think," Tru said. Then she picked up her little plant and gave it a small peck on one silk leaf before tucking it into her shopping bag.

The shop had just cleared out when Nick called. "Can you meet me at the funeral home?"

"Not at the moment," Kaylee said. "Mary is having lunch, and I'm not going to interrupt her."

"Soon as you can, then. I'll be there." He hung up before she could protest any further.

To Kaylee's relief, once Mary came back to the front counter, she was fine with Kaylee leaving again. "Your morning away clearly did you a lot of good, but now you're tense again. So go ahead." She flapped a hand dismissively, then gave a teasing smile. "And tell me how Reese's presentation goes."

Kaylee flushed. Mary had assumed her desire to leave was prompted by Reese's presentation. It felt deceitful to let her go on thinking that, even though it wasn't what she planned to do at all. But she couldn't betray Nick.

"Oh, don't look so stricken," Mary said. "I won't tease you any more about Reese. Go do whatever you have planned. I won't say a word." She mimed turning a key against her lips.

Since Kaylee couldn't think of a reasonable excuse to leave

Bear behind, she snapped on his leash and headed out of the shop. "You be good," she told him as they drove over to Akin Funeral Chapel. "I'm not sure how the Akins are going to feel about my bringing you along."

Bear simply wagged his tail, confident as always.

She parked at the funeral parlor and took a few deep breaths to calm her nerves. As soon as she'd opened her car door, she spotted Giles and Thelma's son, Jay, crossing the parking lot toward her. "You need to come with me," he said as soon as he was within earshot of her.

"I have Bear," she said.

"That won't be a problem." Kaylee found Jay's unusually clipped manner interesting. Was he upset about something or simply playing the part in Nick's cloak-and-dagger activities? She lifted Bear down to the ground, and they followed Jay.

Jay took her around the back of the funeral home and through a metal door, which led into a room Kaylee recognized. It was Giles's lab, and she'd worked in there before to analyze plant material for the sheriff's department. Nick leaned against the long metal table situated against the wall, and Bear rushed to the end of the leash to reach him. Nick bent to pet the dog and revealed a microscope and the materials to make slides waiting on the table.

"Did you find out anything about the sedan in the parking lot of the ferry?" Kaylee asked Nick.

He shook his head, still petting Bear. "I got there too late. The plate came back to a rental agency from the mainland. That's as far as I could go considering I'm not presently working. It was a long shot anyway. The car could have simply meant one of our summer visitors was meeting someone coming over on the ferry."

"Maybe." Kaylee gestured toward the microscope. "You

have something for me to examine?"

"I have a sample of the trace that was on Felicia's shoes," he said. "It's just dirt to me, but I know you can do magic with dirt."

"How did you get trace from Felicia's shoes?" Kaylee asked, then she caught sight of a very guilty-looking Jay standing in the corner. "I see."

Nick straightened and moved aside to give Kaylee more room at the microscope. "Will you check it out?"

Kaylee peered through the eyepiece, gently adjusting the focus for a clearer view. The soil jumped into sharp clarity, turning from a smudge of dirt to a fascinating mix of crystals, decaying organic material, and plant cells. "This is fairly typical soil for Orcas Island," she said. "But the higher percentage of organic material and plant cells suggests it's come from one of the wooded areas."

"I don't suppose you could tell me which wooded area?" Nick asked.

"Maybe if I had samples from every wooded area on Orcas Island, I could narrow it down." Then she thought of the sample of soil Jessica had collected for her from the bathroom sink in the coffee shop. "Hold on."

Kaylee grabbed her purse and rooted for the tiny sample. She quickly made up a slide and examined it. She went back and forth between the two slides. "I believe both of these samples came from the same location."

"What is that second one?"

Kaylee told him about finding the dirt in the sink in the restroom at the bakery. "This second sample may have come from William Tomlinson's shoes. I think he was standing on the sink to reach the window, though I have no idea why."

"But maybe this William Tomlinson knows," Nick said, his voice hardening. "And I am going to go find out."

"Nick, don't do anything foolish," Kaylee started, but Nick stormed past her and out the door. Kaylee felt a sick twist of worry. Had she just sent her friend into real trouble?

15

"Could you please save the slide that's on the microscope?" Kaylee asked Jay. "Label it 'bakery,' and keep it safe. It might be important later."

Jay stepped up to the microscope. "And the slide of trace from Felicia Lewis's shoes?"

"No need to save that one," she said. "It wouldn't be admissible, and the sheriff will already have his own samples from Felicia's shoes. But the fact that the two slides match could be important. I'm not sure." She bent to pick up Bear. "Thanks for everything. I have to go."

"Try to keep Nick out of trouble," Jay said. "He's a good guy."

"I'll do my best."

She dashed to her car. Nick was already gone, but Kaylee was fairly certain he'd gone to the campground. She hoped Reese would still be with the Learners on Location group. Surely he'd be able to talk sense into Nick if necessary.

The drive passed in a blur of worry that Bear seemed to sense. He didn't even perk up when they entered the campground. "Sorry, Bear," Kaylee said. "I didn't mean to make you worry too. We're going to go see friends."

Bear didn't look convinced, but his tail twitched in a near wag.

Kaylee remembered Pepper's comment that the best thing about their campsite was that it was near the restroom, so she crept along the narrow campground road until she reached the small lot closest to the bathroom. Along the way, she peered into each lot but didn't spot Nick's car. "Maybe I overreacted," she said softly. She hoped she had.

As soon as she set Bear on the ground, he perked up and strained at the leash, sniffing. His enthusiasm helped Kaylee feel a little better, but she knew the knot in her middle wouldn't loosen until she saw the Learners on Location presentation was uneventful. At least, she hoped that's what she'd see.

She had just started down the trail to the closest campsite when a hand reached out from the brush and grabbed her arm, dragging her off the trail. Kaylee saw immediately that it was Nick, but she smacked him on the shoulder anyway. "How many times do I have to tell you to stop surprising me?"

Nick shushed her as Bear jumped up on his shin happily. "You two are going to ruin everything. What are you doing here?"

"Making sure you don't do something that could put you out of a job," Kaylee hissed. "You can't just charge into trouble."

"I'm not charging into trouble. I'm surveilling. Or I was until you decided to rush in and 'rescue' me." He added air quotes around the word *rescue*.

"How was I supposed to know that?" Kaylee asked. "You didn't exactly come across as a calm professional when you stormed out of the funeral home."

"You could have trusted me."

"It's a good thing *I* trust you, Nick," a voice said from the path. "Or I might wonder what's going on."

Kaylee recognized the voice. With her face flaming from embarrassment, she pushed through the brush to join Reese, Bear following. With a sigh, Nick came too. Bear seemed torn between which one of his two favorite men to jump on, so he just barked with joy and ran around in a circle.

Reese knelt and rubbed the dog's head, looking up at Nick. "You want to tell me why you're hiding in the bushes?"

"Not here," Nick said, then nodded at Reese. "It's good to see you back on the island."

"It's good to be back." Reese's expression became serious. "I'm so sorry to hear about Felicia."

"You and me both," Nick said.

All three turned at the sound of more voices farther down the trail. In moments, most of the Learners on Location kids ran out to meet them.

"I knew I heard Bear," Carter said, smirking at Pepper. "Told you."

"I didn't argue about it," Pepper replied with an eyeroll.

"You're not leaving already, are you?" Carter asked Reese, then he grinned at Kaylee and Nick. "You guys should come see the cool stuff we made."

"I'd like that," Kaylee said.

The teens herded them back toward the campsite, where William and Jenna were talking in low voices near a line of tents. The leaders stopped their conversation as soon as the group rejoined them.

"I thought you were going," William said to Reese.

"I ran into Nick and Kaylee," Reese answered. "I decided to come back with them so the teens could show off their wood-working skills."

"We made stools," Pepper told Kaylee. "Now we don't have to sit on the ground out here or on some half-rotten log crawling with bugs."

"There were just a few ants on that log," Carter said.

"A few?" Pepper screeched. "I saw fewer ants in *Legion of Fire: Killer Ants*."

Carter was clearly stunned. "You saw *Legion of Fire*? I love that movie."

Pepper rolled her eyes, which was apparently her usual way of communicating with Carter. "You would. I saw it because I have brothers who are as weird as you."

"Okay," Jenna said. "Enough fussing. I thought you guys were going to show off your projects."

That got the teens back on task, and Kaylee admired each stool as it was enthusiastically presented to her. She noticed Nick throwing suspicious glares toward William, but the deputy still made a point of complimenting each stool. Once they'd properly appreciated each creation, Pepper bounced on her toes and asked, "Are you guys going to stay for s'mores?"

"Yeah, we're *finally* getting to have them." Carter and the rest of the teens turned to glare at William.

The leader held up his hands in surrender. "Hey, I was just trying to get you kids to eat healthy."

Jenna giggled. "I don't care much about healthy, so I smuggled back chocolate, marshmallows, and graham crackers from my last trip into town."

"Jenna is our hero," one of the teen boys called out as the others cheered.

"So, are you guys going to stay?" Pepper asked.

Nick smiled. "I do like s'mores, but I need to run into town. How long until you're going to start toasting?"

"Not until after dark," Jenna said. "A fire is more fun after dark, and even *I* think we should eat supper before stuffing ourselves with marshmallows."

"I'll be there." Nick directed his firm tone toward William, who gaped at him in surprise, clearly catching the aggression in the remark.

"I'm sure Bear and I can come back too." Kaylee shot a pointed look at Reese. "How about you? Don't you think s'mores would be fun?" She wished she could beam her intent into his head. She wanted Reese to be there in case Nick needed a calming hand.

Either Reese got the hint or he just liked s'mores. "I'm sure I can get away. It's a good thing I made myself a stool too." He scanned the campsite, then grinned at Nick and Kaylee. "I guess you guys are stuck with the buggy log."

"Thanks a lot, buddy," Nick said.

Kaylee laughed, knowing full well Reese would never make her sit on a log when he had a stool he could loan her. If there was one thing she was certain about, it was that Reese Holt was a gentleman. She turned to the kids. "What are you guys going to do until then?"

"Practice tracking," Carter said, and the others echoed their agreement. "Nick taught us a lot about tracking, and we've been practicing. I saw deer tracks twice."

"Well, you guys can hunt up muddy tracks and grosser stuff all you want," Pepper said. "I'm going to stay here and read." She beamed at Kaylee. "Miss Mary loaned me one of the shop's books on flower arrangement. I'm almost done with it. If I finish, I can send it back with you tonight."

"That sounds good," Kaylee said. Then she told the teen about the popularity of her arrangements. "I'll bring you the money we owe you when I come back."

Pepper positively beamed, and several of the other teens congratulated her. Kaylee was warmed by the way the kids were so supportive of one another. She heard a fair amount of unkind remarks about young people, so she was glad that this bunch had proven to be compassionate and kind.

Finally, Kaylee, Reese, and Nick headed back toward their vehicles. Kaylee was glad Nick didn't insist on staying to interrogate William, though she suspected the questioning had only been postponed, not canceled.

"You two are going to have to tell me what all the sneaking around was about," Reese said as they reached his truck, parked near Kaylee's SUV. "But I have to run for now. I promised to go fix a leaky pipe at the Northern Lights Inn as soon as I finished up here. I really should have been there by now."

"Maybe we can catch up tonight," Nick said.

Reese nodded and turned to Kaylee. "I'll be glad to share a s'more with you later. I have perfect toasting technique."

"Ha," Nick said, his face finally looking more like his normal lighthearted self. "You know I'm the toast master."

"Only if you like char," Reese said.

"I guess we'll just have to wait until tonight to find out who is the toast master," Kaylee said.

"See you tonight." Reese swung open the door of the truck and hopped in.

"Where are you parked?" Kaylee asked Nick. "I didn't see your car."

He gestured through the trees. "There's an overflow lot that way."

Kaylee peered down the trail in the direction he pointed. "Bear and I will walk with you. I know he'd like a chance to do a little more sniffing before we head back to the shop."

"And you want to make sure I leave, instead of going back to shake William until he tells me why his shoes had the same trace evidence as Felicia's," Nick said.

"You know there could be a lot of reasons for the similarity in soil," Kaylee said. "Even if the trace came from this campground, that hardly means Felicia was here to see William. It's the most tenuous of connections."

Nick huffed. "Yeah, I know." He ran his hand through his hair, making it stand on end. "I guess I just feel like I should be doing something."

"You know what I think, Nick?"

"What?"

Kaylee took a deep breath. "I think you're throwing yourself into this investigation to keep from feeling your grief over Felicia's death. I don't think you're ready to deal with that pain, so you are distracting yourself with something else, even though you've been told not to."

Nick stared at her in surprise. He looked like he was about to protest, but then his shoulders slumped. "You might be right, at least a little. I just . . . I can't believe she's really gone, you know? I feel like we could have had something really good, and it's not fair that we didn't have that chance. I'm worried I'll just fall apart if I let myself truly feel it." His jaw tightened. "And I don't feel like I deserve to grieve her until her killer is brought to justice."

Kaylee couldn't argue with that. She put a comforting hand on his arm. "I understand. Just make sure that when this is all over, you process your grief. Otherwise it'll just eat at you forever. And remember, you have friends who care about you. We'll help you through it."

He gave her a small smile. "Thanks, Kaylee."

Kaylee stood at the edge of the lot and waved as Nick pulled out, honking his horn. Then she turned back to the trail. "Poor Mary," she said to Bear. "She's going to wonder where we are."

Bear's only comment was some enthusiastic snuffling of a nearby tree. She tugged him gently back to the path, but then let him lead. She had reached the end of the trail near the lot when someone stepped into her path, making her jump.

"Pepper!" Kaylee put her free hand to her chest. "You startled me."

"Sorry. I just need to talk to you about something, something important." Pepper shot a glance over her shoulder. "I'm not sure what to do about it."

"You're not in any trouble are you?" Kaylee asked, alarmed.

Pepper shook her head. "But I don't want to—" She stopped abruptly, and then a huge smile appeared on her face. "I loved helping out at the flower shop. You're the best."

"Pepper?"

At the sound of a man's voice, the teenager's attention snapped across the parking lot. William stood at the end of the trail leading to the camp, his hands on his hips.

"Yeah?" the teen responded.

"I thought you were going to do some reading," William said, crossing toward them. "You know you're not supposed to run around on your own. When you passed on going on the hike with the others, that meant staying at camp."

"I'm *going* to stay at camp." Pepper's voice was full of typical teen exasperation. "I just had to go to the bathroom."

"Then why aren't you there?" William asked.

"Because I saw Kaylee and Bear." The teen knelt and patted the dog. "I wish I had a dog."

"Bear's really nice," William said, "but you need to run on to the bathroom and return to camp. Kaylee probably has other places she needs to be and other things she needs to attend to."

"I'm going, I'm going." Pepper gave Kaylee a last unreadable look, then trotted toward the bathroom.

William walked the rest of the way to where Kaylee was standing. "I'm actually glad I caught you," he said. "I wanted to ask if you, Nick, and Reese might rethink coming out this evening. The teens have begun to open up and talk around the fire in the evening. We're building trust, and I'm not sure having strange adults there will facilitate that."

"We made a promise to the teens," Kaylee said. Her voice came out colder than she'd meant it to, but something about this man had unnerved Pepper and stopped her from saying something important. "And I don't think it would *facilitate* trust for the teens to think adults casually lie to them. Unless you're planning to tell them that you asked us not to come."

"No, I wasn't planning to say anything like that," William said stiffly.

"Then we'll see you tonight for s'mores." Kaylee gave him a bright smile.

William frowned and took another step toward her. Bear growled quietly, clearly feeling that the group leader was close enough. William scowled down at him.

"Hey!" They turned to see Pepper standing in the lot with her hands on her hips. "I'm heading back to the campsite now. You going to walk back with me so I'm not attacked by a squirrel or something? I'm not supposed to wander around alone, you know."

"I'll be right there." William gave Bear a last frown, then joined Pepper. They headed off down the trail to the campsite. Kaylee watched him go, suddenly wondering if Nick might not have been so far off course after all.

16

Kaylee hurried into the flower shop with Bear in her arms. "Sorry I was gone so long."

Mary smiled at her. "It's not a problem. We've been busy, though. You'll find five new orders on the list. I haven't started on any yet since this is the first time the shop has been without customers since you left."

"Now I feel doubly guilty." Kaylee put Bear on the floor. "Why don't you take the rest of the afternoon off? I can handle anyone who comes in and start on some of the orders."

"Are you sure?" Mary asked. "I don't mind staying."

"I'm sure."

Mary's smile turned mischievous. "Well, Herb did say he'd finally go with me to the funeral home if I got off early today. I bet he thought that couldn't possibly happen two days in a row. He's in for a surprise."

"I could still go with you after we close the shop, if Herb would rather not." Kaylee cringed when she remembered she already had plans. "Not today, though. I promised to go make s'mores with the Learners on Location kids. But we could go tomorrow."

"You're a dear for offering, but making these decisions with Herb was always my goal. I know they're tough, but I'll feel so relieved when they're all done."

As soon as Mary left, Kaylee scanned the order list while pouring herself a cup of coffee. She saw Bear watching her, his head tilted to one side. "I know. It's late in the day for coffee, but I'll need the energy to power through this list before we head back to the campground."

After a few sips of coffee, Kaylee felt rejuvenated enough to start on the new orders. No one else came into the shop that day, so she was able to work uninterrupted. At closing time, she locked up and returned to the worktable to finish the list. If possible, she wanted to get them all done before heading off to join the campers. Although she was trying to work fast, she still gleaned plenty of enjoyment from picking flowers from the cooler and carefully placing them in each arrangement. Making art from the exquisite work of nature never failed to bring Kaylee a kind of quiet joy.

She was just carrying the last pair of small arrangements to the display cooler when she heard a tap at the shop's front window. The sound startled her, and she had to juggle the bouquets slightly to avoid dropping either of them. She hadn't realized her nerves were on edge until then.

Bear darted to the front door and pranced excitedly. Kaylee set the arrangements in the cooler and rushed over to the door, where Reese was peering in under the *Closed* sign.

Kaylee opened the door. "Is everything all right?"

Reese blinked at her in surprise. "As far as I know. Is there any reason to think it wouldn't be?"

Kaylee blew out a relieved breath. "No. I guess I'm a little paranoid. I haven't felt quite right since seeing Felicia's body." She shuddered at the memory, then held the door open for Reese to enter the shop.

"I'm sorry I was away when that happened." He came in and folded his arms over his chest. "I can't say I'm thrilled with Nick for involving you in this."

"After finding the body, I don't know how I could have avoided being involved. Plus, Nick is my friend, and I'm afraid he'll do something foolish if left on his own."

"So, can you tell me more about what was going on with

Nick at the campsite?" As he asked, he looked down and laughed. Bear was sitting on the end of his foot. Reese knelt down. "I think somebody is feeling ignored."

"He was being unusually patient," Kaylee said, locking the door again. "He didn't bark or jump up, so I guess he thought it was time to be rewarded."

"He's right. I'll pet him, and you talk to me. I want to know everything."

"At first, Nick's prime suspect was Isaac Pine." Reese nodded, as Kaylee had already told him that when they'd talked earlier. "But I examined some trace evidence—soil—found on Felicia's shoes."

"Found by whom?" Reese asked in surprise.

Kaylee thought of Jay Akin's guilty expression but decided not to air her theory. "Nick didn't say, but the soil and plant material exactly matched a sample from the men's room at Death by Chocolate."

"Okay, now I'm confused." Reese stood then, leaving Bear to gaze at him in disappointment. "How is Jess's restroom connected with Felicia?"

Kaylee scooped up Bear and petted him absently as she explained about William's collapse in the restroom and her finding the soil afterwards. "I think maybe William stood on the sink to reach the window. But I don't know why."

"You know that doesn't mean much," Reese said. "If the dirt came from the campground, it just means Felicia might have been at the campground. It doesn't mean William had anything to do with Felicia. Is there anything suggesting he'd even met her?"

"I thought the same thing, which is why I want to keep Nick from going after William." Then Kaylee contemplated her own odd interaction with both Pepper and William. "I do think something strange is going on with William though, even if it isn't connected to Felicia."

"Because he's standing on restroom sinks?"

"That, and because he was acting really strangely after you and Nick left the campground today." She related her experience with Pepper and William. "I think his suggestion that we stay away tonight was a little out of line."

"Unless he's being completely honest, and they really are helping the kids work through stuff during their sharing times in the evenings."

"I'd agree, but this isn't a summer camp for troubled teens. I don't know whether William and Jenna are exactly qualified to serve as impromptu counselors. And Pepper definitely wants to talk to me about something. I'm not going to miss that."

Reese held up his hands. "Hey, I'm not suggesting we skip out on her. I guess I want this to be nothing because I feel a little guilty for leaving you alone at the campsite to deal with William, especially if there's something weird going on."

"It's all right. I don't expect you to be my watchdog." Kaylee held up Bear slightly, which put him high enough to give her a quick lick on the underside of her chin. "I have someone for that, and he's pretty good at it. He made it fairly clear to William that he needed to keep his distance."

Reese laughed and reached out to ruffle Bear's ears. "Yeah, he's a bodyguard and a half. But I'd still feel better if you didn't spend any more time with William alone."

"Yeah, so would I," Kaylee agreed. "Right now, my main interest is Pepper. I want to get her alone so she can tell me what's bothering her. She's observant and bright. It's possible she's seen something we need to know about."

"If I see a chance to help you get time alone with her, I'll take it." Reese glanced around the shop and rubbed his hands together. "Is there anything I can do to help here before we go?"

"I just need to clean up a little. We should probably eat something substantial before we head to the campsite so we're not making a supper out of toasted marshmallows. If you don't mind rummaging in the kitchen, maybe you could fix us a couple sandwiches?"

"Sounds like my kind of job," he said, then he patted Bear on the head. "What do you say, Bear? Want to be my assistant?"

Kaylee set Bear down, and the little dog followed Reese cheerfully into the kitchen while Kaylee went back to the work area to tidy up. By the time she was done, Reese had two thick sandwiches ready on the small kitchen table. He also had poured them each a glass of iced tea. She noticed Bear looking especially pleased with himself, and she suspected he'd accomplished some successful begging before she got there.

As they ate, they made a concerted effort not to talk about Felicia's death. Kaylee appreciated that. Her stomach was nervous enough as she thought of the evening ahead. Something had definitely been bothering Pepper, and that worried her. She hoped the teenager wasn't in any danger.

When they were finally clearing up the kitchen, Reese asked, "Do you want to ride with me to the campground?"

Kaylee shook her head. "I'd like to head straight home to bed as soon as we're done instead of coming back for my car. If I leave the car here, I'd have to come in on my bike tomorrow, and I'm really not sure I'm ready for that yet."

Reese gazed at her with concern. "I don't like seeing you scared."

"I'll get over it. I promise." She looked around the clean kitchen and nodded in approval. "We'd better get going. I don't want Nick to get there long before us."

As it happened, Kaylee spotted Nick's car on the road when they turned into the campground, and they all arrived at the small parking lot near the Learners on Location's site at nearly the same time. Kaylee snapped the leash on Bear and hopped out to meet Nick. "I hope you're here with a cooler head," she said.

"Cool as Christmas snow," Nick said with a smile that didn't quite meet his eyes.

Reese joined them and frowned at Nick. "Kaylee caught me up. You need to stay out of trouble."

Nick gave Kaylee a sideways glance. "This is a hard place to keep a secret, it seems."

"Don't give her that," Reese scolded. "She's worried about you. So am I. And since you dragged her into this, you're lucky she's come along this far."

Nick deflated slightly. "I know."

Kaylee cleared her throat. "How about we all go on to meet the kids so we're not standing in the parking lot like conspirators?"

"Good idea," Nick said.

They walked down the well-worn path to the campsite with Bear in the lead, tugging steadily on the leash in his enthusiasm to see the friendly teens again. To their surprise, they found the campsite empty except for William, who was cleaning out the fire pit. He addressed them without enthusiasm. "So you all decided to come after all."

Bear stopped in his tracks at the man's tone, and Kaylee saw the small dog stiffen. She picked him up before he could start growling. "As I said earlier, we made a promise to the kids. We weren't likely to break it."

At that, William's stance softened. "I'm sure the kids will appreciate that." He gestured off toward the woods behind him. "They're out collecting kindling for the fire." He patted a couple of neatly cut logs wrapped in paper. "I bought these today. I'm not much of a woodsman, so I figured we should be sure to have logs that would actually burn."

"I've made more than a few campfires," Reese said. "Let me give you a hand."

Kaylee wondered if he was truly trying to be helpful, or if he intended to use the time to try to get a read on the other man.

William's smile grew warmer and more genuine. "I'll take all the help I can get. To be honest, you might be better off if I stay out of it entirely. Jenna has been laughing at my fire-starting abilities every night since we got here. I think she's secretly glad that I'm so terrible. I make her look good."

"Letting Reese handle the fire will give us a chance to talk," Nick said.

Kaylee and Reese exchanged glances.

"What do we need to talk about?" William asked, his tone growing suspicious.

"Felicia Lewis."

William gave Nick, then Kaylee a confused glance. "Felicia? That was the name of the girl we met at the ferry, right? The one the kids thought was your sister?"

Nick spoke up before Kaylee had a chance to answer. "She's dead. And you know something about it."

"I do?"

Nick took a step closer to William, almost crowding the man's personal space. "I know about the little stunt you pulled at the coffee shop." When William continued to stare at him, he added, "In the restroom."

Kaylee realized she should step in with more information. "I found soil and plant matter on the edge of the sink. I'm pretty sure a soil sample would show it came from right here. And it could only have gotten on the sink if you'd stood on it. Maybe to reach the window?"

"So why would a nice schoolteacher want to climb out a

window?" Nick asked.

William's expression changed from puzzled to annoyed. He glanced toward the woods behind him again, then back at Nick. "Fine. But this has to be quick before the others get back." He jabbed Nick in the chest with one finger. "And if you mess up this operation, it's going to cost you your job."

Operation? Kaylee stared at William in shock. What was going on?

17

William dropped the log he held and took a step closer to them, speaking in a fierce whisper. "I'm not a schoolteacher. I'm an FBI agent. I came to Orcas Island to find out why the woman you knew as Felicia Lewis was here."

They all gaped at him for a moment. The revelation was as unexpected as the sudden change in his demeanor. Mild-mannered and slightly inept William had transformed into a competent, hard-eyed man Kaylee barely recognized. This was the man who had frightened her earlier near the bathrooms, and it seemed like this was the real William Tomlinson. But she still had questions, so she resisted the urge to back away and spoke up instead. "That doesn't explain what made you stand on a sink in Jess's restroom."

William groaned in frustration. "When I chose this cover, I had no idea it would be so tough to get away from the group to meet with another agent. After all, these are teens. They don't need to be watched every second, but Jenna treats them like kindergartners and expects me to as well. I had to arrange for the other agent to meet me behind the bakery. I intended to slip away while Jenna was placing the order. But it was clear that wouldn't work, so I went to the restroom, thinking I'd maybe find a back door to the bakery."

"The rear door isn't near the restroom," Kaylee said.

"Yeah, I figured that out," William said drily. "Which left me stuck in the bathroom. I tried crawling out the window, but it was too small. So I ended up having a conversation with my partner by sticking my head out the window and talking to him while he hid in the bushes."

William's fierce demeanor effectively killed Kaylee's urge to giggle at the image, or at least let her suppress it. She doubted the agent would appreciate the laughter. "So how did you end up on the floor?" she asked.

"I had to wait on my partner to arrive for the meeting," William said. "The change in location wasn't exactly in the plans. By the time he got there and I'd briefed him, Jenna had already pounded on the door twice and then brought you and the kid back with her. You were all right outside the door. I had to give some kind of reason for me to have been in there so long."

Nick waved away the conversation. "I don't care why you were on the sink. I want to know why you were interested in Felicia. And what you meant by 'the woman we knew as Felicia.' And I'm going to need proof of your identity."

"I should just hand that information over to you?" William raised his eyebrows. "Last I heard, you were a suspect in the murder, maybe even the prime suspect."

Kaylee thought Nick was going to launch himself at William. She'd never seen her friend so angry. His face was pale with rage in the waning light, his eyes glinted, and his jaw was tight. She shot a panicky glance toward Reese. *Do something*, she thought desperately.

As if reading her mind, Reese placed himself bodily between the men and addressed William. "I think you'd better stop playing games. If you're an agent, you're going to need to prove it. And if you know something about Felicia's murder, tell us."

William folded his arms over his chest. "She wasn't who you thought she was."

Before he could say more, they all heard crashing in the brush right outside the clearing. The first of the group of teens clomped out of the woods, his arms full of branches. "The campfire can commence," the boy said jovially.

Nick backed away from William, giving him one last pointed glare before moving to help Reese take the piles of branches from the teenagers. Kaylee could tell from the tension in Nick's body that he wasn't anywhere near done with William. She watched the thin group leader, amazed by his return to acting quietly befuddled. He was certainly good at playing a part. What if he was actually a murderer playing the part of an FBI agent? They still hadn't seen any identification.

More of the young people returned to the clearing. Some carried armloads of sticks, while others sheepishly tossed one or two small branches on the pile next to the fire pit. Bear rushed from one teen to another, earning plenty of pats and ear scratches.

Finally, Jenna walked out with her own armload. "Looks like I'm last," she said as she dumped her wood.

"Nope," Carter said. "Pepper isn't back yet either."

Jenna frowned toward the woods as she dusted off her hands. "That girl can turn a five-minute trip to the bathroom into a half-day event. Her head is always somewhere else. I hope she didn't get lost."

"I'm sure she'll be along soon," William said. "In the meanwhile, we could get the fire going."

Jenna rolled her eyes at William. "I'd better handle that."

"I can do it," Reese offered and began placing the wood in a neat tepee to allow the fire to breathe once he lit it. He started with the sticks the kids had brought, holding back the larger pieces William had showed them earlier. Kaylee divided her time between watching Reese set the fire and watching William. Her curiosity made her almost wish Nick would grab the man and drag him off to get answers.

As they prepared for making s'mores, Kaylee expected Pepper to pop out of the woods at any moment. But the fire brightened the clearing, making it all the more obvious that the woods were getting dark and Pepper still hadn't come back. Something was wrong.

"How come we didn't have a buddy system when we went for wood?" Carter asked, worry pitching his voice higher. "Isn't that what you're supposed to do?"

"I think that's for swimming," one of the girls said.

"Well, it would have worked here too. I'm going to go find her," he announced.

"No you're not," Jenna said. "It won't help anyone if we end up with all of you guys lost out there."

Nick pointed at Jenna. "You stay here at the fire with the kids. I'll take William with me to search. And I'm going to call the sheriff's department and tell them we've got a missing child."

"Teenager," Carter corrected, earning himself a reproving frown from Jenna.

"I know these woods pretty well," Reese said. "I'll take Kaylee and Bear with me to search. Bear knows Pepper, so he might be helpful in finding her."

One of the boys laughed. "So the hot dog is going to be a bloodhound?"

"He might just surprise you," Reese said. He stepped closer to Kaylee. "I'll run to my truck for flashlights. Don't let Nick leave without us."

She nodded, sick with worry for Pepper.

Nick had moved slightly away from the group to make his call to the sheriff's department.

Kaylee joined him, Bear in her arms. The second Nick ended the call, she whispered to him, telling him about her conversation with Pepper earlier, and how William had interrupted it. As she talked quickly and quietly, she was relieved to see Reese returning with the flashlights. "I don't know that William interrupted my talk with Pepper on purpose," she said. "But I thought you should know. She knew something that she wanted to tell me."

Nick stomped across the clearing to William and grabbed him by the arm. "Let's get started on the hunt." He practically dragged William into the woods, with Reese and Kaylee following quickly.

As soon as they were out of earshot of the camp, Reese grabbed William's free arm. "All right. What have you done with Pepper?"

William stared back at him. "What are you talking about? Why would I do anything to a kid?"

"Because she had something she wanted to tell me," Kaylee said. "Something she wouldn't say in front of you."

"I don't know what that could have been." William shrugged. "Maybe she figured out I'm an agent. I wouldn't hurt a kid for that."

"I think it's time you provide some credentials," Nick demanded.

William produced a badge, and Nick and Reese examined it. "The sheriff can verify my identity too. He knows my partner and I are working on the island. We didn't want to keep local law enforcement completely in the dark. Too often, they'll stumble into an op and ruin it if you don't loop them in." He stared pointedly at Nick as he said the last part, making it plain that he thought Nick was doing just that.

"So what is it you think you know about Felicia?" Nick asked, his tone still aggressive and his hands clenched.

"It's a long story," William said, "and you're not going to like it."

Reese cut in. "And as important as the story certainly is, we can't do anything to help Felicia right at the moment. But there is a teenage girl missing in these woods. In the dark. We need to find her. She could be lost or worse, so finding her needs to be our focus."

Nick took a step back, shaking out his hands. "You're right. Can I borrow a flashlight?"

Reese handed him one. "We'll split into two teams, if you two think you can focus on the task at hand."

"Of course," William said. "I'm an agent, not a monster."

Nick nodded grudgingly. "We'll stay on task. The woods are no place for a city girl after dark." He gave William a narrow-eyed glare. "Do you have any tracking skills?"

"You mean in the woods?" William asked. "Not particularly. But judging by your demonstration for the kids, you're the master."

"I get by," Nick replied. "I'll take lead, but if you try to sneak off, we're going to have a problem."

"I'm not going to sneak off," William snapped. "You have the flashlight, and I don't know these woods. I'm not an idiot." And with that, William and Nick headed off as a rather growly team.

"I'm not really good in the woods at night either," Kaylee admitted to Reese. "If you'll remember, I once fell off a cliff around here."

"I remember. Let's hope Pepper didn't run into a problem like that." Reese aimed the flashlight beam at the ground and started off.

Kaylee hesitated. "Should I carry Bear or let him walk?"

Reese aimed the light at Bear, who blinked and turned away when it hit him. "Does he like Pepper?"

"He likes all the kids."

"Do you think he might know her particularly?"

"I don't know." She squatted to take Bear's face in her hand. "Bear, can you find Pepper? Where's Pepper?" She felt a little silly, with the teenager's mocking words from earlier ringing in her head. Bear was certainly no bloodhound, and she didn't even have something of the girl's to offer him a scent to match.

But he barked once as if he understood and started through the woods, tugging at the leash.

"Here goes nothing." Kaylee let the dog pull her along.

"Let's just hope it doesn't involve chasing after a skunk." Reese walked close behind Kaylee, holding the light so it illuminated the ground just ahead of her. They pushed through the brush for a few minutes. All around them, the woods hummed with chirping insects and the rustle of unseen animals moving in the dark.

"Hold on," Reese said abruptly. "I see something." He shined the light just ahead. "Look in that muddy area."

They reached the spot, and Reese bent down to examine a footprint. Bear snuffled at the imprint and wagged his tail.

"Boot tracks," Reese said. "Pepper was wearing some distinctive combat boots, right?"

Kaylee nodded. "She wears them all the time. You think that's her footprint?"

"I do, and I think Bear thinks so too." Reese rubbed the little dachshund's ears. "You're a pretty good tracker, pal. You think you can find Pepper?"

Bear yipped and began pulling at the leash again. They continued pushing through the woods, finding tracks from the boots every time they hit soft soil. "She was heading away from camp," Reese said.

"Maybe hunting for firewood," Kaylee said.

Reese caught Kaylee's arm to stop her. "Look at the tracks now. They're deeper and farther apart. I think Pepper started running."

"Why would she run in the woods? She could trip and hurt herself."

"That's a good question. Come on."

They continued to follow the trail. Reese pointed out more tracks and broken foliage, then held up a hand. "Hold on. That print right there isn't from Pepper's boots." Again, he knelt to examine it more closely.

"Maybe someone else came through here today," Kaylee said.

Reese shook his head. "It partially overlaps Pepper's print and has the same pattern of weight near the toe. Someone else was running." He fixed his gaze on Kaylee. "Pepper didn't just run off. Someone chased her."

18

As Bear continued to sniff the ground around the latest foot-prints they'd found, Kaylee looked anxiously at Reese. "Come on." Kaylee grabbed Bear so they could move faster. "We have to find her."

"I know." Reese pulled his phone from his jeans pocket. "But I need to text Nick with what we've found and the location. If we're going to do the right thing for Pepper, we have to keep everyone informed."

Kaylee fidgeted while Reese typed and sent the message. She knew Reese was right, but Kaylee also knew what it felt like to be chased and afraid for your life. She hugged Bear close.

"Done," Reese said finally. "Let's go." He stepped around Kaylee to take the lead. They'd left the path long ago, and he was better at finding signs of Pepper's trail, especially in the dark. Now that she was behind Reese, it took all of Kaylee's concentration not to trip and fall since Reese's light did little to illuminate her way. She wouldn't dream of asking him to slow down, though. The same phrases ran through Kaylee's head on a loop: *We have to find Pepper. She has to be all right.*

Ahead of her, Reese stopped so suddenly that Kaylee nearly slammed into him. "What is it?"

Reese swept the flashlight beam around them. "I think this is where whoever was following Pepper caught up with her."

Oh no. "What makes you think that?" Kaylee whispered.

"There's a lot of broken brush here. See?" He pointed the light at some of the undergrowth. "And the ground is torn up. There was some kind of struggle here."

Kaylee knelt to examine the ground illuminated by the flashlight. Even she could see that the softer soil in the area was marked by partial and overlapping prints. As she was squatting, Bear jumped out of her arms and rushed to the edge of the lit area. "Bear, hold on."

He stopped, his nose to the ground and tail wagging furiously. Then he looked back at Kaylee and barked.

Reese swept the light toward Bear, and something glittered in the beam. Kaylee hurried over and bent to examine it closely. "It's one of Pepper's earrings. I recognize it."

"Maybe she lost it in the scuffle?" Reese suggested.

"Maybe." Kaylee got out her phone and snapped a photo of the earring in place on the ground before picking it up. She knew the importance of documenting evidence. But the thought that she needed to document evidence about Pepper made her feel sick. "She's a smart girl. She might have left this intentionally so we'd know she was here. So we'd find her."

"Well, it's clear from the prints that Pepper and her pursuer left the clearing together," Reese said, refocusing his light on the area beyond the earring. "They're moving slower and together."

Bear tugged on the leash, eager to continue. "We have to find her," Kaylee said, knowing she was repeating herself but unable to stop. They *had* to find the girl, and she *had* to be okay. Kaylee couldn't accept any other alternative.

They came across a game trail and the footprints followed it, making tracking easier since they didn't have to push through brush anymore. Kaylee was in the lead again as Bear pulled steadily on the leash, certain of the direction. Clearly he wanted to find his friend as much as Kaylee did.

Reese grabbed Kaylee's arm. "Hold up. I hear something ahead."

Kaylee picked up her dog again in case they were coming on Pepper and her abductor. That word echoed in Kaylee's mind:

abductor. The teen was in a captor's hands. And that person might be crashing through the woods toward them.

Bear wriggled in Kaylee's arms and barked once, a sharp sound in the night.

"Shh," Kaylee whispered, putting her hand on Bear's muzzle.

"That must be Bear." The voice that came out of the dark was familiar, but not the one Kaylee had hoped for. First the glow from his flashlight appeared, then Nick came into view with William behind him. Nick gave Bear a pat, but his expression stayed grim. "We cut into this trail just as I heard Bear bark. And I saw the tracks. Pepper isn't alone."

Reese swept his light back down the trail. "We need to find them. Fast."

William offered no comment at all, perhaps recognizing he was on thin ice with a young girl missing, a girl who had been his charge. They continued down the trail. With two flashlights, they were able to move quickly. Much to Kaylee's growing dismay, the only sounds in the woods were their own footsteps.

Finally, the trail they were on opened up onto a small gravel parking lot. The lot was empty of cars, which wasn't surprising as it seemed to be quite a distance to the nearest campsite. "I suspect whoever marched Pepper out here must have driven her away," Nick said, his face mirroring the distress Kaylee felt.

She set Bear down on the gravel and fought the urge to cry. "How are we going to find her now?" she asked softly.

"By figuring out who might have had a reason to take her." Nick turned to glare at William.

William quickly held up both hands. "I honestly don't know. I was here to investigate Felicia. The kids were just part of my cover. I didn't pay them much attention."

Nick stabbed a finger toward the agent. "And that's the

problem. If a real group leader were here with the kids, maybe Pepper wouldn't be missing."

"I think you need to tell us what you know about Felicia," Kaylee said, keeping her voice level and hoping that would help calm Nick. She suspected her friend might be close to punching the FBI agent in the nose. "Pepper knew something, something she wanted to tell me in secret. And since you're investigating Felicia, maybe whatever Pepper knows is related to Felicia as well."

"I don't see how it could be," the agent said with a scoff. "I didn't conduct my business in front of the kids."

"Tell us anyway," Nick growled.

Reese put a hand on his friend's shoulder. Kaylee didn't know if it was for support or to keep Nick from leaping at the agent.

"Fine," William said, taking a careful step away from Nick and crossing his arms over his chest. "In Seattle, the woman now calling herself Felicia Lewis worked for a wealthy architectural firm. This was a company that didn't touch a job unless the client was very, very rich."

"And?" Nick prompted impatiently.

William narrowed his eyes, but he was wise enough not to provoke Nick further. "And she was assigned a client, a wealthy industrialist named Max Glower. Glower apparently liked Felicia's work, or maybe he just liked her. I don't know. I do know he asked for her whenever he had a project and tried to hire her away from her company."

"And she took the job?" Reese asked.

"No, she was loyal to her employer, but she spent increasing amounts of time with Glower. And she began to have more and more access to his businesses and his home as they talked about plans for expansion and new construction."

"And she became romantically involved with him," Nick guessed, his voice heavy.

William shook his head. "As far as we can tell, it was strictly business." He dropped his crossed arms, shoving his hands in his pockets instead. "From what we've gathered, a private individual approached her at some point. This person claimed an interest in bringing Glower down, telling her that Glower was involved in foreign businesses with—I guess you could call them unsavory products and services."

For a moment, Kaylee wondered what kind of products and services, then decided she really didn't want to know. Instead, she glanced around the dark parking lot again, wondering how listening to this story could possibly be helping Pepper. Her sense of helplessness weighed on her until it felt like she could barely breathe.

William continued his narrative. "I don't know how, but the guy convinced Felicia to help him. She stole some information from Glower's home office, information about one of these foreign businesses. Maybe about more than one. I don't know for sure. Whatever it was, it was serious stuff Glower didn't want to get out."

"And he caught her?" Reese asked.

"If he'd caught her then, she'd never have made it to Orcas Island," William said. "But he apparently figured out he'd been tricked and who was behind it. The man who recruited Felicia was killed. At first, it appeared to be an accident, but it didn't take long for the coroner in Seattle to realize it was actually murder."

"And Felicia ran here," Kaylee said. "To hide with an old friend."

William nodded, but Nick spoke up before he could say more. "That doesn't explain what you're doing here. If this was a private individual, how did you get involved?"

"We were called in after the guy's death," William said. "This private individual was someone we knew about, a whistle-blower who doesn't mind breaking the law to expose the wrongdoings of politicians, corporations, even government agencies. It's his acts against the government that put him on our radar. We'd been looking for the guy for years."

"And then he turned up dead," Nick guessed. "And that's how you found out about Felicia."

"That's right. She'd been here for a while by the time we figured out what the dead guy had been working on and who was involved. Once we knew the location, we came over to see if we could find the information she stole."

"Why not just ask her?" Kaylee asked.

"Because she'd been working for a known enemy of the government," William said. "Who knew where her loyalties were? We had to secure the information before doing anything to risk making her run. So I came over with the Learners on Location group and lucked into seeing her on the very first day here."

"Just before she died," Nick said harshly.

William winced. "Clearly we weren't the only ones who tracked her here. Glower must have sent someone as well. We didn't expect that. He shouldn't have our level of resources, and Felicia had done a good job of covering her tracks."

"Because she changed her name," Nick said. "So what was her real name?"

William sighed. "Anna Torres."

"Isaac must have known everything. They've been friends their whole lives," Kaylee said. "He certainly knew she was here under a false name. He might know where she hid the information."

"And we'll probably have to pick him up and sweat him for the information," William said. "Hopefully we'll be able to avoid annoying a family as powerful and connected as the Pines. Plus, my partner and I weren't ready to reveal ourselves. It's possible Glower's assassin is still on the island. The tossing of Felicia's cabin certainly suggests that."

"You know about that?" Kaylee was surprised.

"The sheriff is keeping me up-to-date," William said. "I don't think Glower's man found anything. My partner had already searched, though not so obviously."

"So who's your partner?" Nick asked.

"You don't need to know that."

Nick's hands tightened into fists. He was clearly at the end of his self-control.

Reese stepped carefully between Nick and William. "I think you're mistaken about our need-to-know status."

"Your partner is Jenna, isn't it?" Kaylee asked.

William's surprised laugh died quickly when he glanced at Nick. "No," William said. "As far as I can tell, that annoying woman is the schoolteacher she claims to be. She's certainly bossy enough. And I wouldn't have had to talk to Jenna through the restroom window."

Of course not. Kaylee felt her cheeks warm. She realized the disappearance of the teenager had her so upset that she wasn't thinking straight. "That doesn't mean Pepper couldn't have discovered something about Felicia's case, especially if you're meeting your partner regularly. Pepper is bright. If she figured out what's going on, she might also have tripped over some evidence."

"I don't know how," William said. "As far as I can tell, Felicia never came out here."

"That's not true," Kaylee piped up. "She had the same soil trace on her shoes as you left on the sink. That suggests she came out here at some point. And if she did, then maybe Pepper knows something that has gotten her kidnapped."

William rubbed his forehead, showing the first sign of distress over the situation. "She's just a kid. I do know that Pepper was acting odd all day today. I admit, I was starting to worry that she was catching on to me." He glanced toward Nick and something he saw on the other man's face made him add, "I didn't have anything to do with her disappearance. I'm an FBI agent. I don't snatch kids."

"But you were worried that she'd begun to doubt you," Reese interjected.

"I was. But that just meant I was under more pressure to find out who was after Felicia before Pepper managed to out me. At most, I was watching to make sure she didn't talk to anyone outside the group. But if she seemed to be getting too suspicious, I would have shown her my badge and told her to keep my secret."

"So your sudden appearance when she tried to talk to me this afternoon was intentional," Kaylee said.

"Yes, but I wouldn't have done it if I'd thought the girl actually knew something dangerous."

Kaylee shook her head as the pieces fell into place. "And when you asked me not to come tonight with Nick and Reese, that was to keep us away from Pepper as well."

"Yeah. I know this looks bad." William made a helpless gesture. "But I'm telling you, whoever has the kid, it's not someone connected to me."

"Assuming we believe that," Nick said, "it doesn't change the fact that a teenager is missing. And her disappearance is almost certainly connected to something she discovered, so we need to figure out what that might have been. Why would Felicia have come to the campground, if that's what happened? Could the evidence she stole be here somewhere?"

Kaylee hugged Bear to her, then set him back down on the ground. As far as she was concerned, the only question she was desperate to answer was, "Where is Pepper and how do we find her before something terrible happens?" To her surprise, as soon as Bear's feet touched the ground, he began pulling her across the parking lot. "Bear?" she asked. "What is it?"

"He's been tracking Pepper," Nick said. "Maybe he still is."

"Maybe," William said. "But he can't track a car. Why bring the girl to a parking lot unless you're going to put her in a car?"

Kaylee followed Bear across the dark lot until the dog stopped short and pawed at the gravel. "Can I get a light?" she called back to the men.

Reese trotted over and shone his flashlight at the ground. Something flashed among the rocks. Kaylee knelt down. Lying in the gravel was the second of Pepper's earrings. "She tried to leave us a clue," Kaylee said. "I'm sure of it. Even if one earring came off accidentally, this second one was on purpose."

"You're probably right," Reese said, "but it doesn't give us any insight into where the vehicle went, or even anything about the vehicle itself."

"No," Nick said from close beside them. "But this might." He pointed his flashlight at the rocks, where something glistened darkly. For a moment, Kaylee had a terrified thought. Could it be blood?

Reese stood, adding his light to Nick's. "I think it's oil."

"And it's fresh," Nick said. "Whatever vehicle hauled Pepper out of here, it's got an oil leak."

"So we just have to find one vehicle on an entire island. Assuming the kidnapper didn't just transfer her to a boat." William's voice was skeptical.

"Yeah," Nick said. "And we'll do it if I have to check under every car myself. We're going to find that kid. No one else dies."

Kaylee blinked back a stinging sensation in her eyes. She hoped Nick was right.

19

In the dark parking lot, Nick rounded on William. "You need to tell me everywhere that you and Jenna have taken the kids on this island."

Near Nick's feet, Bear barked at the tone of his friend's voice, and Kaylee quietly shushed him, tugging gently on the leash to call him closer to her. She agreed that compiling a list of spots the group had visited on the island was as good a place to start as any—perhaps Pepper's abductor was one of the people they'd met—but Nick's aggressive demeanor wasn't going to help them focus.

For a moment, it seemed like William was going to argue. Being told what to do by a mere sheriff's deputy obviously didn't sit well with the FBI agent. He must have realized that quarreling with Nick could only end badly, however, because he ultimately gave in. "There aren't too many places we haven't gone with the kids. All over the campground, of course." He nodded toward Kaylee. "To her shop and most of the businesses downtown. The kids had presentations to attend at the florist, the bakery, a fishing boat, and the bookstore."

Kaylee felt a twinge of guilt about the bookstore. She hadn't been by to see DeeDee in days, and she'd intended to look in on both the bakery presentation and the writing lesson DeeDee had given at Between the Lines.

"Which fishing boat?" Nick asked.

William had to think about it a moment. "The *Promise of Spring*. The captain's name is Mel something."

"Mel Cameron," Nick said. "I know the boat."

"So do I," Reese said. "I did some custom work in the cabin, a breakfast nook and new bunks. Mel's a nice guy."

Frowning, Kaylee tried to call up a mental list of the programs they'd planned for the Learners on Location. "I helped plan the week. I don't remember a demonstration on a fishing boat."

"That's because it wasn't on the list," William said. "We had some free time, so we took the kids to lunch on the dock and met the captain. He was really friendly and thought the program was a great idea, so he threw in an offer for a boat ride and fishing demonstration. I figured it would give me a chance to see more of the coastline, so I jumped on it. The kids loved it."

"I wonder if that's when Pepper saw something," Kaylee said. "When did you do that one?"

"Yesterday," William answered.

Kaylee shook her head. "Pepper wasn't with you for lunch yesterday. She was at The Flower Patch."

"That's right. I forgot. Honestly, the kids haven't been my main focus."

"Yeah, we've noticed." Nick's voice was edgy. "Okay, this isn't getting us anywhere. Who knows when or where she made her discovery? Let's focus on people who have behaved suspiciously. And that means Isaac Pine."

"Pine?" William looked at him in surprise. "He's clean. The guy's a Boy Scout. He helps little old ladies cross the street. He definitely doesn't abduct kids."

"But he knew who Felicia really was," Nick answered. "When even people closest to her on the island didn't." Kaylee heard the hurt in his voice then. Felicia hadn't trusted *him* with her secret, and Nick was probably realizing she might not have felt the same about him as he felt about her. "He's the logical one to have sold her out."

Kaylee wasn't convinced. "I don't think Isaac would betray

her. But I met a man who works for the Pine family, Wallace. He clearly didn't like Felicia, and I'm not sure he likes Isaac much either. If he overheard something, I could imagine him making a call to remove her from the Pine property. At the very least, he must have told Isaac's father. I get the feeling that's where his real loyalties lie. And once a secret begins to spread . . ."

"It doesn't stop," Nick finished. "That doesn't change what we need to do. We need to talk to Isaac Pine and his butler."

"That's probably a good idea," Reese said, speaking for the first time in a while. "But I think the first thing we need to do is return to camp." He pointed in the general direction of the campsite. "There could be a witness there. The woods were full of teenagers during Pepper's disappearance."

"They said they didn't know where she went," Kaylee pointed out.

Nick sided with Reese. "Sometimes witnesses don't realize what they saw."

On the return trip through the woods, Bear was the only one who showed any excitement, clearly thrilled to be moving again. Kaylee suspected her dog was going to sleep heavily when they finally got home. She winced at the thought. *Who knows when that will be?*

When they reached the campsite, two deputies were there. Robyn Garcia was speaking quietly to a sobbing Jenna Olsen. Alan Brooks stood near the group of teens, who all looked equally miserable. Both deputies stiffened slightly when they saw Nick, but they nodded at him in greeting. At the sight of William, Jenna left Robyn's side and came over to throw herself on the FBI agent with a sob. William froze and held out both hands as if not sure what to do.

If Nick noticed the tension in his fellow deputies, he didn't react to it. Instead, he walked up confidently and began reporting on what they'd found. Jenna managed to stop crying long enough to turn and listen to Nick, though she still clung to William, who patted her shoulder awkwardly.

"Reese and Kaylee found Pepper's tracks in the woods, along with the tracks of another, unidentified person," Nick said. "Personal belongings, earrings, were found twice—once in the woods and once in a gravel parking lot about a quarter mile in that direction." He took a deep breath before he came to the point. "It looks like someone chased the girl in the woods and eventually caught her. Then she was marched through the woods to the parking lot, where she was driven away."

"No sign of where to?" Deputy Garcia asked.

"No, but we did find some leakage at the spot where the earring was located," Nick said. "Whoever abducted the girl is driving a vehicle that leaks oil."

"That's useful to know," Robyn said, writing it down in a small notebook. "But it doesn't give us any idea of where to start the search."

Kaylee noticed that both deputies made a point of not making eye contact with William. *They know he's an agent,* she realized. *Otherwise they would be asking him questions.* So why had the sheriff told them the big secret?

Jenna began sniffling again, and Kaylee saw William gently disentangle himself from the distraught woman. Jenna stood beside him, hugging herself as if she felt cold despite the warm night.

Nick approached the group of teens standing around the dwindling fire. "Pepper told Kaylee that she had something to tell her, something important. Do any of you know what that was?"

The teens exchanged glances, and Kaylee saw bewilderment on most of their faces.

"She didn't say anything," one of the girls said. "But she's been kind of weird most of today."

"Don't call her weird," another girl whispered fiercely. "She's missing."

The first girl put a hand on her hip. "Doesn't change the facts."

Kaylee turned away from the girls and noticed that Carter had taken a small step away from the group. When she caught his gaze, he flushed.

"Carter?" she said. "Did Pepper mention something to you?"

His flush deepened. "No. I mean, I could tell she was acting weird. She wasn't talking. Pepper is *always* talking. But maybe you could read her notebook?"

That caught Robyn's attention, and the deputy stepped up beside Kaylee. "What notebook?"

"I guess it's a kind of journal," Carter said. "She draws in it a lot and writes stuff too. I was kind of watching over her shoulder while she was drawing a flower arrangement, and she nearly took my head off. I guess that notebook was private."

"Anyone know where it is?" Robyn asked.

"Probably in the tent," one of the girls said. "That's where her cot and her backpack are."

"I'll go get it," Jenna offered. She headed for the tent, but Deputy Garcia stepped into her path.

"No, thank you," the deputy said. She pointed at Kaylee. "Why don't you and Alan go look?"

"Her?" Jenna asked. "Why her and not me? I'm in charge of these children, and before you go violating their privacy, I think I should be there."

"Miss Olsen," Robyn said calmly, "I don't know you, and until we find the girl, I have to be careful not to taint any evidence we find."

Jenna puffed up, clearly annoyed as she pointed at Kaylee. "But won't she taint evidence? She's not a law enforcement officer."

"Yes, but she has experience working with us in an official

capacity. Deputy Brooks will keep her from touching the evidence directly," Robyn replied. "And I trust Kaylee. I don't know you."

Jenna jutted her chin out stubbornly, but she didn't say anything else. Kaylee suspected the deputy preferred a grumpy Jenna over the sobbing version. She knew William would. She handed Bear's leash to Reese and followed Deputy Brooks into the girls' tent. As the deputy flashed his light around, they could see the tent was surprisingly roomy. Though it wasn't tall enough for Alan to stand upright, he only had to stoop slightly when they reached the center. Four cots were lined up with sleeping bags unrolled on them, and beside each cot rested a backpack. Hanging from one wall was an electric lantern, presently off.

"Do you want me to turn on the light?" Kaylee asked.

"The flashlight will do." The deputy shone it across the cots. "Do you recognize any of these backpacks?"

Kaylee pointed to a graffiti-print knapsack. "That one belongs to Pepper. I remember seeing it the day they arrived."

He hefted the bag onto the cot and unzipped it. Holding the flash in one hand, he started to shine it inside but halted with a wince. "I suspect she would rather a man not rummage through her clothes. You look, and I'll watch you."

Kaylee actually smiled at that. "To make sure I don't tamper with evidence?"

Alan rolled his eyes. "Don't you start. You missed the hysteria earlier. That Olsen woman fell apart when we got here, and she got all the kids stirred up with half of them crying. If Robyn wasn't here, I might have made a run for it."

"You afraid of a few tears?" Kaylee teased.

"I'd rather break up a bar fight." Alan pointed at the backpack, holding the flashlight to best illuminate the contents. "So, please, see if the journal is in there."

Kaylee went through the backpack. She found a collection

of shorts and T-shirts. *Pepper must still be in the jeans she was wearing earlier.* She also found a few small shopping bags that contained trinkets bought in town, possibly gifts for family back home. She also found several pens and a pack of colored pencils, but she did not find a notebook.

"Do you think she had it with her?" Alan asked.

Kaylee thought for a moment. "I can't imagine why she'd carry a notebook to gather firewood, but I suppose it's possible if she had things inside that she really wanted to keep private. But it's not the only answer. Maybe it's in the cot?" She was tempted to simply feel around for it, but she didn't want to run afoul of any evidence rules.

"Yeah, that makes sense." The deputy zipped up the backpack and returned it to its original spot beside the cot. He pulled back the sleeping bag to reveal a spiral-bound notebook. "Found it."

Alan carried the notebook out of the tent to the better lighting near the fire. Deputy Garcia took the notebook and flipped through the pages while Brooks aimed his flashlight at it from over her shoulder. Kaylee was fascinated by the skillful sketches on the pages. There were several beautifully executed drawings of flower arrangements, and several rougher portraits of the kids in the program. Kaylee almost laughed at the sketch of Carter, which perfectly captured his personality.

Then Robyn turned the page, and Kaylee gasped softly. The page held a rough sketch of Jenna laughing, but someone had drawn a huge X over the image and printed *liar* across it. Everyone looked up from the sketch to Jenna.

The program leader shook her head. "That's nothing. Pepper threw a fit because I told her she could have her phone to call home. Then I found out she just wanted to call some boyfriend, so I took the phone away again."

"That's not true," one of the girls argued. "Pepper didn't

have a boyfriend. I was talking about my boyfriend, and how much I missed him, and she said she didn't date. She said teen romance was a waste of time and creative energy. It was kind of obnoxious, actually."

"Well, that's not what she told me," Jenna said, her chin out and her tone mulish.

One of the teenage boys piped up. "You know, I saw Pepper when we were out collecting kindling."

"And you didn't say anything?" Nick demanded.

"It was early, right after we went out," the boy said. "Anyway, I passed her and started to say something about how lame it was to pick up sticks like little kids, but Pepper shushed me."

"Did you know why?" Robyn asked.

The boy shrugged. "I figured it was just weird girl behavior. They do stuff that doesn't make sense *all* the time." He jerked a thumb at Jenna. "But the funny thing is, I'd seen Jenna just a few seconds before. Now that I think of it, I think Pepper was heading toward her."

Jenna rolled her eyes. "Coincidence. No one was going in any particular way."

Nick narrowed his eyes and stepped toward the group leader. "Where is that girl? What did you do with her?"

"Have you lost your mind?" Jenna demanded. "I didn't do anything with her. How could I? Where could I possibly have stashed a teenager? In my pocket?"

"Maybe we should take a look at Jenna's rental car," Kaylee suggested. "Just to rule her out. If her car isn't leaking oil, we'll know it isn't the vehicle that took Pepper."

"Fine." Jenna took a couple steps toward the parking area, then suddenly bolted. The deputies took off after her, but the group leader was amazingly quick. She might have gotten away except for Bear. The little dog jerked forward so suddenly he took

Reese off guard and pulled the leash out of his hand. Then he sprinted across the campsite, racing right into Jenna's path. The group leader tripped over the dog and went sprawling, making Bear yelp.

"Bear!" Kaylee yelled, running to him. While the deputies hauled Jenna to her feet, Kaylee scooped up the dachshund and ran her hands over him, checking for sore spots. Bear simply lapped at her chin, not reacting to her gentle prodding. He was all right.

As the deputies held the struggling woman, Robyn said, "Reese, please stay with the kids while we check out the car. Nick, I know you're not exactly on the payroll right now, but maybe you could come with us. William too. I assume you can point out Jenna's car?"

"I can." William's voice was grim, but he seemed a little shocked. He clearly hadn't considered Jenna a potential suspect.

Kaylee followed the others to the parking lot.

William pointed to a small car not far from the bathroom building. "That's Jenna's car. I didn't think it was necessary to rent a second car, but I was glad of it." He smacked himself in the forehead. "I can't believe what a dolt I've been."

"That's for sure," Jenna muttered.

Deputy Garcia searched Jenna, earning some curses from the other woman that didn't sound anything like the cheerful young teacher Kaylee had met at the ferry dock only days before. When Robyn found the keys, she opened the rental car's trunk, and they all gasped. Though the trunk was mostly empty, it did hold a pair of bolt cutters, a roll of duct tape, and another piece of jewelry Kaylee recognized: the thin leather bracelet Pepper always wore, the one she said she'd gotten from her grandfather.

"You put a child in the trunk?" Kaylee's voice was shrill, echoing in the parking lot.

"I don't know how that stuff got in there," Jenna snapped

back. Since Deputy Garcia had cuffed her, she used her head to gesture toward William. "Maybe he put it in there. Maybe he grabbed the kid."

"This isn't the time for games," Robyn said, her voice dangerously tense and quiet. "Where did you put the girl?"

"I've got nothing to say." Jenna closed her lips and smirked.

Kaylee felt her stomach clench with fear. They didn't have time for this. Pepper was out there somewhere, and probably scared out of her mind. She might even be hurt. How were they going to find her?

20

Judging by the clenched fists and angry scowls on the deputies holding Jenna by the arms, Kaylee knew they were as desperate to find a way to get the woman to tell the truth as everyone else. But as everybody glared in frustration at the smirking woman, Kaylee had a thought. Maybe Jenna had already told them where she'd put Pepper.

"Jenna grabbed the girl in her own car," Kaylee said.

William gave her an annoyed glance. "Yes, we all know that."

"No, this is important," Kaylee insisted. "Jenna didn't pass Pepper off to someone else. If she had, Pepper could be anywhere. But Jenna said it herself—she didn't have time to take the girl very far. Pepper must be here in the park somewhere."

"You mean tied to a tree or something?" Alan asked, his voice filled with doubt.

"I was thinking more of an outbuilding." Kaylee met Nick's gaze. "I've been around this park a good bit, and there are several buildings for park workers. What if she used one of those? I think there's a stone structure not far from here."

Nick's face lit up. "I know exactly where that is." He pointed into the woods. "We can reach it down a path through there quicker than using the paved road."

Kaylee noticed that the smirk had slid from Jenna's face, and she felt sure they'd struck on the right place.

"Should I lock her in my vehicle?" Deputy Brooks gestured toward Jenna. "I could stay behind to watch her."

"No," Garcia said firmly. "In case Kaylee's wrong, we'll want her close at hand. But grab the first aid kit, just in case, and get a crowbar too. We may need to force the door."

As soon as Alan had the case and crowbar in hand, they hustled the cuffed woman toward the trail with Nick in the lead. Kaylee glanced back toward the campsite, wondering if she should stay with Reese and the worried kids. With a shake of her head, she trotted after the others. She had to see this through. Pepper would need a friendly face when they found her.

If they found her.

They were on a well-used path, so even with the darkness, it was easier and faster going than their earlier search in the woods. Kaylee whispered a prayer for Pepper's safety as they hurried along as quickly as they dared. Finally, the path let out on a clearing, and they came upon the small stone building. It had a heavy wooden door and high windows that were little more than horizontal slits in the stonework.

Bear barked and began wriggling to get out of Kaylee's arms. She set him down and he rushed at the door, barking wildly. No sounds came from inside, and Kaylee had a sudden fear that Pepper could be badly injured. Or worse.

A shiny lock hung in the hasp of the door, but it didn't take Deputy Brooks long to pry the fixture off the door. They hauled the thick door open and every flashlight shone inside.

Pepper sat on the floor in the only empty spot, surrounded by shadowy shapes of boxes, bins, and various tools. She was thoroughly bound with duct tape, with a strip across her mouth. Even half covered in tape, the relief and anger in the teen's face were easy to see.

Kaylee rushed to the girl's side. Bear jumped into Pepper's lap and starting chewing on a strip of tape.

Nick bent down and picked up the dog. "No slobbering on the evidence, buddy."

Bear looked positively insulted to be removed from the role of rescuer.

Kaylee carefully pulled the tape away from Pepper's mouth. "Are you okay?"

"Yes." The girl whipped her head around to glare at Jenna, who stood in the doorway in Deputy Brooks's firm grasp. "*She* locked me in here!"

"Yeah," Nick said as he began helping Deputy Garcia carefully cut the tape that bound the girl. "We figured that part out."

Pepper smirked at him. "Well, did you figure out this part? She called some guy to come and get me—to come and *kill* me."

"I don't know what that kid is talking about," Jenna said.

"Did you hear a name?" Robyn asked. "Anything at all to help identify the person she called. How did you know it was a man?"

"I could hear him through the phone a little," Pepper said. "He was yelling. He told Jenna she was going to ruin everything, and he wasn't coming to bail her out. She didn't like that, let me tell you. She was spitting mad when she stuck me in this shed."

Nick stormed over to Jenna. "So this partner—is that who killed Felicia? Or was it you?"

Jenna narrowed her eyes at him. "I don't know what you're talking about."

Deputy Garcia cut through the last bit of tape around Pepper, and Kaylee and Robyn lifted the girl to her feet.

Bear danced around happily.

"Oh," the teen said, wavering. "My legs fell asleep." She bent down and rubbed her calves, then scooped up Bear, giving him a hug. "Thanks for being so happy to see me."

Bear gave her a kiss on the chin.

While Kaylee watched this, she remembered something. "I

might know something about her partner."

"Like what?" Nick asked.

"I saw Jenna arguing with someone in the ferry parking lot. She told me a story about the guy making a pass at her, but the argument seemed to go on for some time. It didn't seem like someone she'd just met." Kaylee turned toward Jenna. The glare the woman gave her sent a cold chill down her spine. The real Jenna was nothing like the part she'd played.

"What did the man look like?" Robyn asked.

"I'd seen him before. He came into The Flower Patch and bought an arrangement, then gave it to Jess at Death by Chocolate. I thought it was a sweet gesture at the time, even though it puzzled me a little." Kaylee described him quickly.

William gasped. "That's not her contact. It's mine. He came to the island ahead of me to scout things out. He must have been following Jenna. She probably confronted him so he pretended to hit on her. He never told me about the incident, but since it would have made him seem questionable, it's not that surprising."

"Does this guy drive a blue sedan?" Kaylee asked.

"Yeah, so?"

"So maybe he was playing both sides," Nick cut in. "Someone in a blue sedan tried to run over both Kaylee and Felicia. Considering their strong physical resemblance, I think Felicia was actually the target both times. And with you tied to the kids, your partner would have plenty of unsupervised time."

"I think we're done here," Deputy Garcia said. "We've got to get all the kids somewhere safe, and we need to take Pepper's statement. And we need to take Miss Olsen to talk to Sheriff Maddox."

"Where will you take the teens?" Kaylee asked. "You can't leave them out here without an adult, especially since it turns out they never had a true group leader."

Nick smiled. "If I know you and Reese, I'm betting you two can take care of a few teens."

"Normally I'd love to," Kaylee said. "But under the circumstances, I'd like to go with Pepper." Then she smiled. "I may have another idea."

As they all walked back to the campsite, Kaylee called Mary, who delightedly offered to put up the girls in the group for the night.

"I'll come get them right now," Mary said. "And you can bring Pepper by when she's done at the sheriff's department."

"That won't be necessary," Kaylee said. "I'll take her to my place when she's done."

Pepper, who was still carrying Bear, gave her a warm smile when she heard that.

When they returned to the campsite, the teens cheered at the sight of Pepper and piled on her in a group hug. As they'd thought, Reese quickly volunteered to take the boys home with him. "My place isn't huge, but if the guys don't mind bringing their sleeping bags, we can throw some of the cots into my truck, and they should be comfortable enough."

The boys all agreed to the idea, but their enthusiasm was a quiet one. Worry had exhausted everyone. Kaylee bet they would all sleep well that night.

At the sheriff's department, Pepper proved to be a great witness, reciting everything in detail and never changing a single element of her story on repeat questions. She did insist on holding Bear the whole time, but clinging to him was the only sign that the horrible experience she'd been through had rattled her.

Pepper had seen Jenna making frequent phone calls, and she'd been irritated by that since the teens weren't allowed their phones. "I decided I wanted to know who she was talking to all the time. I figured it was her boyfriend or something," Pepper said. "And I guessed I'd hear something I could call her on, and then I could make her give back everyone's phones. But the more I heard, the more it sounded bad. Like, *illegal* bad. That's when I thought I should talk to Kaylee. She seemed like she'd know what to do."

"And the crossed-out drawing?" Sheriff Maddox asked.

"That's when I was just mad at her, thinking she was a hypocrite about phones and boyfriends. But then she got mad at the guy on the phone. She said it was all his fault for trying to stick her with a body in the first place. That didn't sound like boyfriend talk."

When the sheriff was finally finished with Pepper, the teenager was almost stumbling from exhaustion. Kaylee took her straight back to the cottage and put her in the guest bed.

"Can Bear sleep with me?" Pepper asked. She'd finally set the dog down when they got to the cottage, but Bear was loyally sticking close to his new friend. He'd already jumped up on the bed with the girl.

"He'd love that," Kaylee said, thinking Bear knew more about offering comfort than any human she knew.

Kaylee took Pepper to The Flower Patch with her in the morning. She was surprised to see only one other teenager there, a shy girl who reintroduced herself as Claire, making Kaylee feel vaguely guilty that she hadn't made more effort to learn all the teens' names.

"Where are the other girls?" Kaylee asked Mary while Claire and Pepper busied themselves on the sales floor smelling DeeDee's goat milk soaps.

"They didn't think hanging out in a flower shop all day sounded like much fun, so Megan and Nina are helping out at Between the Lines, and Brittany is next door with Jess. Those girls definitely know what they like." Mary nodded toward Claire and whispered, "I think she wanted to stay with me because last night freaked her out."

"Pepper too," Kaylee said softly. "She slept with Bear. He's the best four-legged therapist I know."

"Good dog," Mary said, giving Bear a treat. This time, Kaylee didn't scold her at all.

As the day progressed, Kaylee noticed that Pepper immediately took up the role of helping Claire get to know the shop and the chores associated with it. As soon as the girls had the shop swept and dusted until everything gleamed, they were off to the worktable. Kaylee was glad to see that working with the flowers seemed to give the teenagers the same comfort that it did for Kaylee.

As for herself, Kaylee was fidgety all day. She knew the investigation must be progressing, and it bothered her more than a little to be shut out. It wasn't that she wanted to get in the way of the sheriff's department, but there were so many unanswered questions, and she couldn't set them aside. Was William's partner also Jenna's partner? Which of them had killed Felicia? And where was the evidence that Felicia had brought from the mainland?

By late afternoon, she was nearly ready to climb the walls. "I'm going to take Bear for a walk, if that's all right," she said to Mary, then headed out with her friend's blessing.

As Kaylee and Bear headed down the sidewalk, she spotted someone she recognized—the young man who bought a flower for his wife every day. He was pushing a wheelchair with a thin, pretty woman sitting in it. He waved at Kaylee, and she walked over.

"This lady owns the florist shop where I get your flowers," he told the young woman, then turned to Kaylee. "This is my wife, Penny."

Penny smiled up at Kaylee. "They are beautiful. A lovely part of a lovely visit to the island."

"I'm so glad to meet you," Kaylee said. "We've wondered who inspired such romantic gestures."

Penny's cheeks pinked, which brightened her pale face. "I'm a lucky woman," she said softly.

As her husband gazed down at her in clear adoration, Kaylee had to agree.

Kaylee and Bear returned to the sidewalk in front of The Flower Patch just in time to spot Nick approaching from the other direction. Kaylee waved him into the shop ahead of her. "I hope you have news for me."

"News, and thanks. I've asked a lot of you lately—probably too much."

"You're my friend and you were in pain."

For a moment, the old Nick surfaced in the smile he gave her. "You're the best friend I could ask for."

Kaylee grinned back at him. "That's saying a lot. I hope you're not in too much trouble with the sheriff. He has to know by now that you didn't exactly stay out of the investigation."

"I'm not at the top of his nice list," Nick said. "But solving a murder is, so I think I'll be fine. We searched that other fed's room and checked his phone records. We found more than enough evidence that he was Jenna's partner as well as William's. When we confronted him with that, he spilled everything."

"Which was?"

"He had been part of the task force trying to bring down the industrialist, but he was taking money from the bad guys to build himself a nice little nest egg for the future. Except Felicia saw him take an envelope of cash. Even with his undercover excuse, he knew he wouldn't be able to cover that up, so he killed Felicia to save himself."

"He wasn't under orders to assassinate her?" Kaylee asked.

"Apparently not." Nick leaned against the counter. "But at least we know who killed Felicia. He admitted to leaving a dead bird at Felicia's cabin, hoping to scare her into revealing where she was keeping the evidence. It didn't work, so he decided to just kill her. He admitted to trying to run you down, thinking you were Felicia."

"There's a warm, fuzzy thought," Kaylee said wryly, then shivered. "To think he was in the shop, and that he gave Jess that arrangement he bought. We thought he was so nice."

"Just part of an act, trying to make sure nobody figured out that he abducted Felicia and took her out to the woods near the campground to kill her." Nick's voice broke a little, but he shook it off. "Anyway, even with him in custody, we don't have anything to help bring down the bad guy who got this whole thing started. Without the evidence Felicia stole, the real villain is going to come out of this scot-free."

"At least you know Felicia's killer is going to pay," Kaylee said.

Nick nodded sadly. "Yeah, but it doesn't feel finished. I couldn't protect a woman I was falling in love with. And now I can't even help take down the thing she feared." Then he perked up slightly, apparently thinking of something. "Oh, they tracked down the anonymous source that put Felicia on the island. The one that clued in the FBI."

Kaylee raised her brows. "Oh?"

"It *was* Wallace. You were right about Isaac. All he wanted was to help keep Felicia safe."

"So Wallace called the FBI?" Kaylee asked. "Not the bad guys?"

Nick shook his head. "He thought Isaac was harboring a

fugitive and that it would reflect badly on the family. So he called someone he knew in the bureau, and that's how William and his partner ended up on the island in the first place. And what ultimately put Felicia in danger."

"In that case, I'm glad Felicia's bird bit Wallace," Kaylee said. "So who searched Felicia's cabin? Wallace or William's partner?"

"Wallace," Nick said. "He thought he was working for the FBI when he did it. Apparently William's partner chatted with him. And since Wallace disliked Felicia and was certain her murder was going to destroy the family, he took out his temper on the cabin. Though, that came back to bite him in a different way, since Isaac had him clean up the place as soon as the sheriff released it."

"Good for him." Kaylee thought of the horrible mess in the cabin. "Too bad the parrot wasn't loose so he could defend the whole cabin. He certainly did a good job on his own domain." Then she startled. "The poor bird. I haven't been back out there. He must be hungry."

"I'm still on leave to the end of today, so I could drive you out if you can get away," Nick said.

"Just let me tell Mary."

As Kaylee explained to Mary and the girls about the bird, Pepper fidgeted nervously and asked if Bear could stay with them. Clearly his job of furry therapist wasn't quite finished. Kaylee agreed.

When she and Nick got to the cabin, Kaylee was relieved to see the bird still had plenty of water and even some untouched food. "At least I didn't let the poor thing suffer," she said.

Nick stood well away from the cage since the bird squawked whenever he walked close. "He certainly doesn't like men much."

"Can you blame him?" Kaylee asked. "He witnessed Wallace tearing up everything Felicia owned. And he probably misses her."

"Something we have in common," Nick said.

Kaylee gave him a teasing smile. "Maybe you should adopt Hero."

"Not a chance. Isaac said his sister volunteered to take the bird. Sounds like she is keen on the idea of an attack parrot. Isaac said it'll give him one more excuse not to visit his sister. That family has issues."

"Many do." Kaylee turned back to the cage, wondering if she should try to clean it. The parrot had been plucking at the newspaper in the bottom of the cage, even though a wire panel kept him from tearing it up too much. Then she peered closer at the spot where the newspaper had torn. Underneath, she saw printed computer pages. "Nick, you need to see this."

Nick edged closer carefully. The bird eyed him menacingly. "You don't think . . ."

"She might have realized it was the safest place in the cabin," Kaylee said. "With someone on guard all the time."

Nick called Sheriff Maddox, who arrived shortly with Deputy Garcia and an eager Agent Tomlinson.

"I'll handle this," William said. Before anyone could warn him, he made a grab at the tray. He'd barely touched it before the parrot dove at him, pecking the back of William's hand hard. "Ow! Stupid bird."

"He doesn't like men," Kaylee said. "Maybe Deputy Garcia should try."

Soon Deputy Garcia was speaking gently to the cranky bird while she donned thick gloves. She pulled out the tray that held the papers as the bird watched her intently. They found that a thin layer of newspaper covered pages and pages of printed financial ledger.

William flipped through the pages. "This is it," he said, nearly laughing with relief. "This is what we need to put this case to bed."

Kaylee leaned over close to the cage. "Good bird," she murmured. "You're a hero after all."

The cranky parrot nodded, his whole body bobbing with the action. Clearly he agreed.

Kaylee smiled, and her grin grew as she thought about Bear back at the shop with Pepper, giving the teen some much-needed emotional support while she processed her traumatic experience. *I guess what they say is true,* she thought. *Heroes really do come in all shapes and sizes.*